JIMMY
The Pickpocket
of the Palace

DONNA JO NAPOLI

~ JIMMY ~
The Pickpocket
of the Palace

illustrated by JUDITH BYRON SCHACHNER

DUTTON CHILDREN'S BOOKS · NEW YORK

Thanks go to Michael Durkan
for his aid as a linguistic consultant
and for his wonderful smile.

Text copyright © 1995 by Donna Jo Napoli
Illustrations copyright © 1995 by Judith Byron Schachner
All rights reserved.

Library of Congress Cataloging-in-Publication Data
Napoli, Donna Jo, date.
Jimmy, the pickpocket of the palace / by Donna Jo Napoli;
illustrated by Judith Byron Schachner.—1st ed.   p.   cm.
Sequel to: The prince of the pond. *Summary:* Jimmy, the froglet
son of an enchanted frog-prince, tries to save his pond from the evil hag
and, in the process, finds himself transformed into a human boy.
ISBN 0-525-45357-1 [1. Frogs—Fiction.   2. Fantasy.]
I. Schachner, Judith Byron, ill.   II. Title.
PZ7.N15Ji 1995   [Fic]—dc20
94-26089   CIP AC

Published in the United States by
Dutton Children's Books, a division of Penguin Books USA Inc.
375 Hudson Street, New York, New York 10014
Typography by Adrian Leichter
Printed in U.S.A.
First Edition
3   5   7   9   10   8   6   4

To the memory of my father

D.J.N.

To Donna Jo,

with love and gratitude

J.B.S.

CONTENTS

JIMMY
The Pickpocket
of the Palace

ONE

~ The Horse ~

I HOPPED TOWARD the cattails at the south end of the pond, a few leaps behind the blue heron. Within moments the heron would enter the shallows, and her jerky steps would stir up all sorts of delicious morsels. I leaped again, knowing I shouldn't be this close to the bird; she could swallow a young frog like me in one gulp. Danger made my skin tight, but taking chances was part of life. And I was clever at hiding. Plus I was quick, and the bird walked on slow, stiff legs.

My tongue tightened, ready to zap whatever

tiny edible creatures escaped the bird's bill. That's when I felt the vibrations in the ground. An instant later the heron gave an alarm call of four hoarse squawks and took to the air.

I leaped in a circle, I was so excited. The rhythm of those vibrations could mean only one thing: the gallop of a horse—yes! I was wild about that horse. I hadn't seen him since last fall, but I could picture him clearly—mane tossed in the wind, tail high.

He was an amazing animal. First of all, he had four legs that were all the same length. Like a newt. Except the horse's legs were long like the heron's—this fellow towered over any creature I'd ever known, even the hag, even the man on his back. He was the color of a cool, cloudy day. In fact, the first time I saw him, last autumn, I thought he had formed out of the fog.

I wanted to ride that horse. I'd dreamed about it all winter. I wanted to wait while the man slipped off the horse's back and then hop up. But I wouldn't sit on the horse's back, like the man. I'd sit smack-dab on the top of his head, between his ears. I'd see everything. It would be like flying. Face into the wind, like the great blue heron.

As soon as the horse came into sight, I leaped for the water and swam hard. I knew he'd circle the pond, then head for the east shore, where he always went.

"Where you goin', Jimmy?" called out my brother in a sleepy voice. It was early spring, and we'd been out of hibernation only a couple of days. The pond was full of groggy amphibians.

"The horse is back," I shouted, without slowing down.

"Great," yelled my brother from behind me now. I heard the almost silent noise of a frog slipping into water, and I knew he'd gone to spread the word. Everyone liked to watch the scene on the shore. But they came for the man. I went for the horse.

I was exhausted but triumphant when I got to the shore. I'd beaten the horse. I hung in the water, my legs dangling down, my eyes and nostrils out in the warming spring air. Soon the other fawgs dotted the water, careful to stay among the water iris shoots, their mottled green camouflaging them. We fawgs looked indistinguishable from frogs except when the males croaked—we croaked with only our left vocal sac, a trait we inherited from Daddy. But we called ourselves fawgs when we were together 'cause that's what Daddy used to call us before he disappeared. Daddy said lots of things in his own strange and wonderful way. And he did lots of things in his own strange and wonderful way. When we called ourselves fawgs, we felt safe and special, like we used to feel when he was here.

The thought of Daddy made all three chambers of my heart hurt. He'd been gone since last fall, and every fawg in the pond felt his absence. Even Mamma, who insisted it was in a frog's nature to be a happy soul, had a tinge of sorrow in her voice ever since Daddy left.

But this wasn't a moment for gloomy thoughts. The horse was coming. I moved closer to the shore in anticipation. The fawgs were careful not to bob out ahead of me. I was their leader, by natural inclination. Mamma said I was hatched bold.

The horse slowed to a trot, then pranced a few steps and stopped. I paddled my forelegs in the water, imagining what it would be like to prance. The horse gave one long, high-pitched whinny. The man looked out over the pond. "Hello out there," he called. He got to the

ground and paced the shore while the horse nibbled at the chamomile beyond the mud. The man finally stopped, right where I knew he would. "Here." He knelt and drew a circle with his finger. "Right here." He stood up and stamped his foot emphatically. "Yup, here."

The circle was in the same place he'd drawn it every time he'd visited. It was the place where I'd once waited for my death. I was trapped in a bucket by the hag. But the other fawgs saved me. Sometimes I liked to remember it; it sort of gave me a thrill. Other times I just got nervous at the memory and had to go off and stuff myself with water sow bugs.

It was uncanny: The man hadn't been present when the hag caught me in her bucket, yet he seemed to know about it. He had shown up for the first time back at the well near the palace on the very day Daddy disappeared. After that, he'd come regularly to the pond all last fall. He was somehow connected to us, and I thought I knew how.

The man took a small gold box out of his pocket. He turned it over in his hands. I knew all about that box. The first time the man had visited our pond, he had searched through the mud and around the bottoms of the hawthorns, half frantic. Finally, he shouted, "Eureka!" And he held up the crystal ring.

That ring belonged to the hag—and it could do magic. Daddy had battled with the hag the time I got caught in her bucket. In the middle of the fight, her crystal ring flew off, lost. But when the man came to the pond, he found it. That was another thing he knew that he shouldn't have known—that the crystal ring was there on the shore somewhere.

The man had washed the ring in the pond water. Then he'd taken that box out of his pocket and dropped in the ring. Afterward, each time he came, he took the box out of his pocket and turned it over and over. But he never opened it.

Now the man tossed the box in the air a couple of times; then he put it back in his pocket. "Where are you?" he said loudly, as though someone besides us pond folk were listening to him. He squinted his eyes and seemed to be searching among the irises. "I know you're out of hibernation by now."

The way he said it, it seemed almost as though he was talking to us. We stayed perfectly still.

He paced again. Suddenly he stopped dead in

his tracks. He took off a strap of leather from his waist, held it by the tip, and tapped the shiny metal at the other end of it on a mound of mud.

Snap. The turtle's head darted forward, and the shiny metal disappeared in its mouth.

"Aha! I knew you'd like my belt buckle." The horseman jerked the leather strap upward, and the huge snapping turtle hung from the tip, its jaws clamped tight, all four legs scrabbling at the air. The man looked closely at the dangling turtle. "Don't I know you?"

The dreaded turtle glared at the man. I shuddered at the power of those jaws. And I admired the man, both for knowing the turtle was hidden there and for not being afraid of it.

The turtle kicked so hard, it spun.

"Yup, look at that crack in your jaw. You're the one that declared war on me. You tried to eat me."

At that I almost laughed. This man thought a turtle had tried to eat him. Was he crazy? No turtle would try to eat a man. Not even a giant snapper like that one. Oh, it would snap and break a finger off, but it wouldn't eat him.

"And I just bet your stomach's stuffed with frogs." He tapped the shell on the turtle's underside. The thought of all the frogs inside that stomach made me sick. The man's face looked sick, too. "Yup, I bet it is," he said slowly. "I should take you home and turn you into soup. But I could never eat you, knowing you were fat from frogs." He scratched his head.

Then he smiled. He picked up a stone and put it near another stone. Quickly, he walked around the shore picking up stones with one hand and holding the leather strap with the turtle dangling from it in his other hand. He piled the stones at least a foot high. Then he balanced the turtle on its back on top of the pile. "It'll take you a good hour of jiggling around to right yourself now. And here's what you're going to think about as you struggle. Listen up good." He put his face close to the turtle, so close I got worried the turtle might snap at his nose. He spoke firmly: "You're not going to eat frogs anymore. Hear that? No more frogs. You tell every turtle in this pond. I'll be back to check up and, believe me, you don't want to see what'll happen if any of you have been eating frogs."

He took a knife out of his pocket. I held my breath. The man raised his arm and, with one swift slash, he cut the leather strap, leaving the turtle with a mouthful of metal.

The turtle flailed his legs in rage and spit out

the metal. I watched his wicked tail whip futilely
from side to side, and I wanted to jump for joy.

The man laughed again. "You really are the
King of Dumb." He picked up the metal. "I got
a bargain here, and it didn't even cost me my
belt buckle." He rolled up the leather strap and
put it and the metal in his pocket.

Then he looked out over the water once
more, and his face became instantly solemn.
"Hey, everyone out there. Things are hopping at
the palace, so I won't be back for a while." He

hesitated. "Will you miss me?" Then he said softly, "I miss you."

I was surprised by this sort of talk. What could it mean?

The man stood silent for a moment. Then he said his usual parting words: "Take care of each other. You're in charge of the pond now." He went to the horse and led him to the water.

The horse would take a drink now. A long, slow drink with those blubbery lips that had weird spiky hairs coming out in all directions. This was always the best part of the man's visit. The horse clumped along and stopped with his front hooves in the water. He leaned his neck down. I could feel the heat from his nostrils. It would be easy to leap between those ears, if only I weren't in the water. My hind legs needed something solid to push off against. I moved closer, out from the safety of the reeds, until my hind feet touched bottom. My eyes fixed on that lock of hair between the horse's ears. It beckoned to me.

"Hey." The man scooped me up out of the water. I gulped pondweed in my surprise. "You better watch out. Chester could have swallowed you." He looked me over carefully. "You look like . . ." He shook his head. "Nah, it's not possible. You're just an ordinary frog—someone else's little frog."

I could have jumped free. I was a champion jumper. But the man didn't seem threatening. After all, he'd told the turtle not to eat frogs. That had to be a sign he was good. Still, I stayed on the alert.

The man carried me to a big rock where I'd often sat last summer with Daddy and Mamma. He put me down, and I felt the tension inside ease away.

Then he did a nice froggy thing. He squatted near the rock with his fingers touching the ground and stayed very still. After a few moments his fingers dug into the mud, and he tossed a giant slug onto my rock. "Enjoy," he said. He walked back to his horse, climbed on its back, and made a click out of the side of his mouth. The horse took off.

I watched them disappear. My skin still tingled from the touch of a human hand. And my heart raced oddly, almost like horse hooves. I'd come so close to leaping on the horse's head. So close. Just one moment more, and . . . Who knew when I'd get a chance like that again? I ate the slug slowly, taking consolation in its savory pungence.

Sploof! Gracie landed on my head and bounced off. "Sorry," she said with a giggle. Gracie wasn't one of my sisters. And she wasn't among the smallest young frogs, either—so that bump on the head hurt. Gracie had taken to following me around last fall. She seemed fascinated by us fawgs and insisted on being adopted into the family. Mamma had named her Gracie out of hope, I was sure, 'cause Gracie was certainly the least graceful frog I'd ever watched. "You almost got eaten," said Gracie.

I didn't answer. I was sure neither horse nor man ever even thought of eating me, but I didn't tell Gracie. Some arguments weren't worth getting into.

"I worried about you." Gracie's tongue darted out, and a mite disappeared into her mouth. Most frogs didn't worry about each other. That was one of the things that made fawgs different from frogs. But Gracie had taken on fawglike ways, and her voice rang with sincerity. "If you were gone, I'd miss you."

If I were gone. Oh, if only I'd leaped in time, I might be gone now. Yes, I loved our pond, I truly did. But there was so much to see out there. So much that the birds talked about that I'd never seen.

"You're dreaming again, aren't you?" Gracie nudged me with her foreleg. "You were thinking about the horse, weren't you? You're always saying how great he is."

"I'm going to ride that horse someday."

Gracie looked astonished. "Why on earth would you want to do that, Dreamer?" Gracie always called me Dreamer 'cause once Mamma had told Gracie I was her dreamer. Gracie liked to copy Mamma.

I stretched the toes on my right foreleg and spoke nonchalantly. "Maybe I'll take you along for the fun."

Gracie shook her head hard. "Thanks anyway." She looked out toward my huge family—which had become her family, too—frolicking like proper young frogs in spring. Some of them had even dared to go up onto the shore close to the struggling turtle. Now they leaped over each other in a celebration parade around the pile of stones under the turtle. Gracie's smooth green skin shimmered with excitement. "Come join the game while it lasts. Snapper's going to turn himself over before long. Hurry." She flipped off the rock.

I watched briefly; then I plunged in. After all, it was spring, and leapfrog was one of my favorite games.

~ The Hag ~

IT RAINED THAT night and all the next day. Frogs came out from under logs and stones, from burrows dug into the shoreline, even from the mud at the bottom of the pond. Zillions of us. We played and splashed and dove and leaped gleefully. There's nothing like the feeling of being wet to the core. Even the newts joined in. They're usually grumpy at the start of spring because their skins are thick from being on land all winter. But with all the rain, the newts' skin had thinned out fast, so they felt good. And a few stray toads had already come back to the pond in preparation for mating. I don't generally have much to do with toads, but when they're in a mating mood, they aren't too bad. The pond rocked: It was an amphibian riot.

That night we poked fun at the spring peepers with their high, piping whistles. We green frogs wouldn't start singing for another month; we let the peepers be the first to announce spring. They sat amidst the tender red wintergreen leaves and the fuzzy gray puffs on the pussy willows and sang till I thought they would pop. The wood frogs felt challenged and added their hoarse clacking to the din. I fell asleep, grateful that I had the pleasant voice of a green frog, sweet like a chickadee's. With that voice I could even entrance the horse if only I got another chance.

When the sun came out the following morning, it felt good on my sensitive skin as I snoozed. I stretched out my hind legs so I could absorb more of the warmth. Ahh. Little did I dream the sun brought with it the worst thing on earth: the dreaded hag.

Gracie made the discovery. She came swimming so fast she slammed into me before she could stop herself. "Jimmy," she said urgently.

Whenever she called me Jimmy, I knew something bad was afoot. "Jimmy, the hag's back."

I didn't waste time asking. I swam in the direction Gracie had come from, my eyes focused on the shore. And there she was, the hag I feared more than anything else in the world.

She was on her hands and knees in the thick mud, almost exactly in the same spot my horse had been in two days before. "Where is it? It should be right here. Right here." Her face was close to the ground, but even so, I could see her profile. And she had a nose! The last time she'd been to the pond was the time she'd caught me in her bucket and she'd had a battle with Daddy. That's how she lost her nose. Daddy had clung to it so tight that when she pulled him off, her nose pulled off, too, and the bullfrog came along and ate it. Yet here she was again, with a nose. But wait; there was something odd about the new nose.

I swam closer for a better look.

The hag jumped up and scowled at me.

I dove and circled over to the irises. My brothers and sisters were already bobbing in and out among the shoots, silent in their fear.

"I saw you, froggy." The hag hopped first on

one foot, then the other. I wondered how she managed that. My hind legs always moved in unison. The hag shook both fists at the spot where I'd disappeared. "You did this. One of you dirty frogs took my nose, and there's not a potion in the world that can fix it." She petted her nose slowly. "But that's okay. All I need is the ring. With that ring I can turn anything I want into anything else." She petted her nose faster now. "I'll find my ring. The ground isn't frozen anymore, so I can dig easily. I'll find it." She flung her head back, and suddenly her nose swung sideways. "Yeegad!" She straightened it and held it tight to her skin. And now I knew what the problem was. Her schnoz was made of wood. It was a fake.

She dropped down on all fours again and raked her fingers through the mud. "Where is it?" She flung mud this way and that. She scrambled and thrashed and mushed the mud between her hands. Then she sat back on her heels and slumped. "It's lost," she wailed. She threw herself facedown in the mud.

We waited. But the hag didn't move.

I came out from the reeds slowly. Was the hag dead? I swam toward her. She never moved a muscle. I sat on the edge of the waterline now.

The hag was just a few long leaps away. Her back didn't seem to rise or fall at all. I leaped.

And as I leaped, the hag's left hand shot out. But she grabbed too late; her hand closed right behind me.

"Eccch!" came the scream.

My skin crawled. It wasn't a hag scream; it was a release call—the scream of a captured female frog. I leaped and leaped, around the hag and back into the water with a splash. Then I came up quickly and watched in horror.

The hag held Gracie in her left hand. "Tormenting me, are you?" She squeezed Gracie, who gave another scream, but quieter this time —it was clear the hag's grip was taking its toll. The hag lifted Gracie high over her head and shook hard. "I can squish the guts right out of you."

Without thinking, I came up onto the shore and leaped at the hag. I smashed against her knobby knee.

"What's this? A suicidal froggy? Don't you know I can squash you to slime?" The hag stomped her right foot. I jumped away just in time and leaped behind her. She twirled and stomped her other foot. I leaped behind her again. She twirled and jumped at me with both

feet. I leaped right through her legs. She bent over to see where I went and fell on her head.

Gracie flew through the air and went plop into the pond.

I leaped for the water.

The hag slowly stood up. She picked mud globs from her thick brows and jutted her chin out toward the pond. "I always knew there was something wrong with this pond. You aren't normal froggies. Normal froggies don't attack. You're crazy. Berserk. And you think you can get the best of me." She straightened her schnoz. Then she touched her hands together at the fingertips and narrowed her eyes. "You've got my ring, don't you? I know it now." She pointed one long, crooked finger out at the pond. "You, froggy. The one who made me fall. You're going to stand up tall and go get my ring and bring it right here to me. Wherever you are, in this very second I am putting a spell on you." She closed her eyes. Then her voice came out high and keening: "Out of the gloomin', become a human."

The amazing words echoed in my head as I stayed frozen, hidden among the iris shoots. I was about to become a human! Me, Jimmy the fawg. I hardly dared to breathe. The idea was unimaginable.

The hag opened her eyes and looked everywhere. Then she glared. "Where's the stupid human? What's wrong? Criminy! How could I forget? That spell needs more to complete it." She loped in a circle, flailing her hands as though she were trying to take off in flight. "If I had my ring, I could do it. Blast it! Without that ring, it takes a princess to complete the spell. Where am I going to find a princess stupid enough to do my bidding on that dirty froggy?"

I looked down at myself. She was right: I was still a frog. And she was still angry. What would she try next?

The hag stopped and shook her fists again. "I'll get that ring. I'll get it if I have to search every inch of the pond." Her words came out in big explosions of air, like thunder in a storm. "And once I get it, this wooden nose will become a nice new live nose. You hear that?" She shouted out to the pond. "You think you've won, you bits of sauce flavoring. But I'll be back."

The very water around me vibrated with the trembling of our fawg bodies. I could see the hag's evil eyes shining with fury.

"I've got it," she screamed suddenly. "I'll make a potion—a potion to dry up water. It won't be hard to make one up. I'll experiment. It never takes me more than three or four days to perfect a potion. Ha! And as soon as I've got it right, I'll be back." Her cackle rose up high and piercing. "I'll sprinkle it over your reeds right there, and I'll dry up every last drop of water from your precious pond. Then I'll have a froggy fry. Ha ha ha ha! If that ring isn't here on this shore the next time I come, you're all doomed." She spun around and ran off, her ugly laugh trailing behind her.

I dove, with dozens of my siblings diving around me. We raced to the bottom of the pond, to the exact spot where Gracie had gone under. And there she was, Mamma on one side of her and young fawgs gathering all around. We sat silent, waiting for our hearts to stop pounding.

Finally, I spoke up. "We've got a problem."

"We sure do," said Gracie. Her weakened voice shook with anger. "You almost got me killed."

"Me?" I was astounded. "You're the one who followed me."

"You're the one who went up on the shore near the hag."

"You didn't have to . . ."

"Hush," said Mamma. She looked at me with steady eyes. "Jimmy, your curiosity won over your common sense." Her voice was harsh.

I knew she was right. But it wasn't my fault Gracie had followed me. Plus I was the one who had saved her by making the hag trip. I looked at Gracie, ready to argue my point, but now I saw the fingerprints of the hag deep in Gracie's side. She would hurt for hours. I hung my head.

"Everyone pay attention. We have a much

greater problem now," Mamma said. "The hag
will come back and dry up the pond." Mamma's
voice was heavy with sadness. "It's been such a
wonderful home." She looked across us slowly.
"The next home will be even better, though."

"What?" yelped Gracie. "We're going to
leave the pond?"

The fawgs sat in stunned silence, looking at
each other. They shook their heads. No one
wanted to leave our home. No one had ever even
dreamed of such a thing. No one but me. That

was it. "No," I half shouted. I swam over and sat right by Mamma, excitement growing inside me. "The hag wants her ring, nothing else. So all we have to do is give it to her."

"We can't give her what we don't have."

"I can get it."

Mamma stared at me.

"I'll get it from the man."

Mamma shook her head. "Oh me, oh me, oh me, oh me. Impossible. I'm taking us back to my old pond. You'll get to see cows. Cows are like short, fat horses, Jimmy. They graze all around that pond."

"Forget cows," I said. "I'll get the ring. All I have to do is go to the palace, near our old well. That's where he lives, I'm sure. I'll sneak in and find the gold box and bring it back." And I can find a way to get a ride on my horse, I thought. A ride through the countryside. I can see everything there is to see in life.

"No," said Mamma. "You heard what the hag said. With the ring she can turn anything she wants into anything else. We can't give it back to her. She'll do terrible things."

"What could be worse than her drying up the pond?"

Mamma blinked hard.

"How could you bring back the box, any-way?" said Gracie. "How could you carry it?"

"In my mouth. Daddy and Mamma carried dozens of us fawgs in their mouths from the well back to the pond when we were froglets. I can carry that little box easy."

Mamma shook her head. "You'd have to go inside the palace, where the man lives. If you got caught . . ."

"The man is no enemy," I said.

"All men are enemies," said Mamma.

"Not this man." I paused for effect as I looked at my family. "He's a friend of Dad-dy's."

"What!"

All the fawgs gasped.

I nodded firmly. "That's why he told the tur-tle not to eat us."

Gracie spoke in a tiny voice. "How do you know?"

"Think about it. He knew the ring was in the mud. He talks to the pond as though he knows we're listening. And he appeared for the first time on the very day Daddy disappeared. Re-member? The woman in the green dress was about to eat me and then Daddy jumped up in her hand and the next thing we knew Daddy was gone and the man was there. I bet he hid Daddy from her." I stopped. There was only one possible conclusion. I spoke slowly, my heart swelling with each word. "I bet he talks to Daddy."

Everyone was silent for a long moment.

"I think you're right," came a voice from behind me.

"I agree," came another voice, trembling with hope.

Fawgs in all directions nodded their heads. The hope was contagious. "That's right. It's right." Everyone looked at Mamma.

Mamma stared off through the murky bottom water. Down here there were still isolated ice crystals. The delicate fairy shrimp floated by. She swallowed one. We all took her cue and swallowed shrimp greedily.

"Mamma," I said between bites, "think what would happen if the hag dried up the pond. Think of the other pond creatures. The fish and the newts. They couldn't escape."

"We're frogs. It's not our job to think of them."

"Maybe it is," I blurted out without realizing what I was about to say.

No one said anything.

But suddenly I was sure of it. Suddenly it all made sense. "Mamma, we're in charge of the pond. That's what the man says every time he comes to the pond. He's talking to us." I gulped. "He's telling us Daddy's wish."

Mamma stared at me. "Oh me, oh me, oh me, oh me," she muttered at last. "It is the kind of thing Daddy would say."

All the fawgs nodded. Their eyes shone bright with the memory of Daddy.

Mamma's eyes were still fixed on me. "Do you really think you can get the ring, Jimmy?"

"I know I can." And I could. I had to. For Daddy. For my daddy, wherever he was.

Mamma swallowed one last shrimp. "All right, Jimmy. You have a couple of days at least before the hag returns. Go. Do your best. But be careful." Then she whispered, "And try to find out where Daddy is."

"I will," I whispered back.

"And if you do see Pin . . ." Mamma hesitated. "Tell him Jade sends her love." Pin was what Mamma called Daddy. Jade was what Daddy called Mamma.

My throat thickened. "I will."

THREE

~ Cashmere ~

THE SUN WAS lazy. It dawdled its way across the clear sky, coddling the new shoots everywhere. I could go a long way without needing to wet my skin if the weather didn't change. I might be able to make it all the way to the palace without a dip. All the way to the man. And maybe, just maybe, to Daddy.

I knew exactly how to get to the well by the palace. All frogs know the way back to the spot where they were hatched. I moved with assurance.

A red-winged blackbird skimmed by and startled me. Blackbirds are no danger. But I was grateful for the reminder: I hadn't been alert enough to predators. I leaped along more cautiously, listening and looking.

And thank heavens. For now that I paid attention, I could feel the vibrations in the ground of a scuffle not far ahead. I leaped to the closest bush, backed in under it, and dug with my hind feet until I was halfway into a burrow.

A large brown toad landed with a splat in the dirt just beyond my bush. It flattened itself out and hugged the ground in that way that only toads have. It was scared beyond thought. I stayed still as a stone.

The skunk was upon it within seconds. It slapped the toad into the grasses and rolled it with its nose. I knew what it was doing. The skunk would roll that toad until the grass scraped off all the toxins the toad's fear had sent to its glands. Then he'd chomp him up. I shut my eyes.

I heard the crunch of toad bones in a skunk mouth. I shivered and opened my eyes. It was better to watch and stay wary and ready, no matter how sick I felt. I remembered the hag putting the spell on me—she had spoken magic words and tried to turn me into a human. If I were a human now, I could scare the skunk away with my size alone. But the spell hadn't worked, and here I was, just the right size for a skunk mouth. I braced myself.

The skunk didn't look around. He finished his meal and waddled off.

I waited, staring at bits of toad innards, my enthusiasm for the trip gone. After a long while, I came out and looked around. The world was minus one toad, but otherwise nothing had changed. That's how things were. If it was your time, it was your time. I leaped again, the longest, fastest leaps I could manage.

The sun was higher now, and I was warming up. I could feel the olive green on my back change to a paler green, which would reflect the sun's heat better. It would also match the color of the new grasses. All in all, a good change. I was still nervous from the skunk episode.

Hunger stirred in my stomach. I stopped and sat very still.

A black beetle scurried across the dead leaves at the foot of a beech tree. It was shiny, fat, and altogether attractive. It reminded me of a flat-bottomed whirligig beetle, the type that skates on the water's surface. Except it had mandibles sticking out in front. I'd never eaten a bug like that before. But if I swallowed him bottom first, those mandibles couldn't grab hold of my tongue. I took one flying leap and gulped down the bug. I waited. I felt a pinch in my gut. I vomited out the bug.

I leaped along again, still hungry. I passed mice racing in a game of tag. I passed an empty snakeskin, recently shed. My own skin was tight. I would molt soon, like the snake. I sat still and waited, all systems on alert. But the snake was apparently nowhere near. Of course it wouldn't be. The mice would never have frolicked so joyously if danger was near. I continued on my way, feeling more lighthearted with every leap.

Song sparrows called to each other from clusters of pink flowers in the elder trees. This was the first spring of my life. Last fall Mamma told us how we'd wake after the winter to a world of colors. Now her words came alive. I decided I loved spring. And of course I loved summer and fall. It was only winter that wasn't terrific—I resented sleep. There were so many more fun things to do.

I was glad I'd taken this opportunity for world travel. The globe was glorious.

I knew I was close to the well long before I saw it. I sensed it somehow. I leaped faster and farther now.

I hopped up on the stone wall of the well and looked in at the cool water. Memories of carefree tadpole days danced before my eyes. This was the place Mamma and Daddy had spawned us last summer. We had slithered around each other in mass profusion in that very well. Just sitting there, I easily satisfied my hunger from the gnats buzzing over the water. Yum.

I dove in and relaxed. When I came back up onto the wall, I surveyed the grounds. I was behind the palace. My beautiful horse was nowhere in sight. No one appeared to be awake. At least there was no one in the backyard and no one hanging out any of the holes on the sides of the palace. That was good. I could sneak in and take the gold box with the hag's ring. Then I would hide the box while I went back and followed the man around until I found out about Daddy.

I thought of my daddy last summer, leaping gracefully from rock to rock, racing through the water, then basking in the sun. Afraid of no one.

Strong and proud and wonderful. I'd find out whatever I could about him. I had to. And no matter what I learned, it would be better than not knowing.

I blinked my eyes and focused on my first task: getting into the palace. On the west side lay a group of flat stones with plants in round clay boxes at the edges. Beyond it was a hole in the house at ground level.

I leaped through the grasses, my heart leaping just as hard inside my chest. Everything lay ahead. Everything important. Within seconds, my feet hit the hot stones. Before I knew what was happening, the monster was upon me.

"*Ffffssss!*" The monster swiped with one paw. I felt my right hind leg rip open. "*Ffffssss!*" The monster pounced. I leaped with all my might and barely managed to make it into a plant box. I wriggled and dug with my good leg and worked my way partially under the wet roots. "*Fffsss!*" said the fat, furry monster. It swatted the plant, and thick, leathery leaves cascaded around me. They were dark, shiny green with smooth edges. They landed heavily on my head and forefeet. The monster hesitated. Its cold, unflinching eyes looked at me, and I wondered why it didn't jump up into the box and rip me to shreds. It could. It easily could. The tip of the monster's tail twitched back and forth. Its whiskers jerked. *"Ffffssss!"* It put both front paws up on the box edge. Then it hesitated, as though it couldn't figure out what to do next. Maybe I was lucky and this was a very stupid monster.

It looked back over its shoulder through the hole into the palace. I nestled backward in under the roots as far as I could go. I was breaths away from death. Within seconds, even an idiot monster would figure things out and leap up into the box. Then I'd be a late-morning snack. I thought hard. A frog's only weapons are intelligence and speed. But my right leg ached so bad that I knew I couldn't move fast. The only thing was to outwit this monster. Maybe I could scare him. I tried to look ferocious. I snapped my mouth several times. The monster dropped its head forward and gaped at me.

"Cashmere!"

The monster looked over its shoulder again and quickly took its front paws off the box edge.

A small human female in a flouncy dress shook her finger at the monster. "Cashmere, you bad cat. What are you doing on my patio?

You're not supposed to come near my things." She stooped and picked up a leaf. "Look at the leaves you knocked off the jade plant. And that's the yucky prince's favorite plant. You're really in trouble now." She wrinkled her nose and made a terrible hooting noise: "Ahhhchooo." Then she bent over and peeked under the plant. "What are you after? Have you got something trapped?"

I stayed very still, the ferocious look fixed on my face.

"Why, it's a frog." The human moved her face closer. "And his leg is bleeding." She straightened up and put both hands on her hips. She hooted again: "Ahhhchooo."

My heart stopped. Was she about to attack?

"You're a very bad cat," she said to the monster. She made the hoot again, even louder: "Ahhhhchooooo!" Then she touched her fingers to her cheek and smiled. "I thought it was going to be another awful day, when all anyone can talk about is Marissa's wedding. But now, instead, I've got a frog." She rubbed her hands together. "A sick frog. I'll clean off that leg and smear on some camphor and wrap it up with a white cloth." She reached under the plant and dug me out.

I leaped, but her hands surrounded me, and all I could do was struggle in her grip.

She held me up high and inspected my leg. "That must hurt." The human stuck out her lips and spoke slowly. "Mother used to kiss my boo-boos." She seemed to think about that a minute. "I wish you weren't so slimy. But I know that scratch hurts, poor frog." She closed her eyes. Then her big, hot lips made straight for my leg.

I froze.

And zap! Bam!

I was sprawled on my back on the stone floor. That position felt awful. The human was sprawled out beside me, emitting little screams. I tried to leap away, but everything was different. Everything was wrong. My skin went dry and my head was heavy and my legs, all four of them, flopped every which way, banging into the human as she stood up. I knew the monster cat would pounce any second. I thrashed around like a fiend and finally managed to get into something like a squat.

Cashmere arched his back and fluffed out his fur and spit. Then he backed away and ran off. Cashmere was small. And, oh, I was gigantic! I towered over the cat!

The human stared at me. "Who are you?" She shook her head and rubbed at her nose, which was now red and drippy. "You can't come on my patio naked like that." Then she pointed at my leg. "And you're bleeding." She hesitated. Then she put her hands on her hips. "What did you do with my frog?"

The human's words made no sense—I was the frog. Was I so gigantic she couldn't even tell what I was? This was crazy. But she was right about one thing: My leg was still bleeding. I could feel the dribble of blood. And, oddly enough, it was hot. I looked down to assess the damage.

Yikes! Instead of my smooth, shiny skin with the dark bars on the legs, I saw pale, goose-bumpy skin with hair. I'd never seen hair on a frog. Plus my leg was shaped wrong. The thigh was nice and muscular like it should be, but the calf wasn't long enough. And the foot at the end —oh! What had happened to my lovely webbed foot? At the end of my leg was a short, skinny foot with five separated toes. I quickly looked at my other leg. The same. I looked down at my stomach. Instead of nice golden yellow, I saw that same pale greenish white that was on my legs. My froggy brain could hardly think. I had to get away. I hopped. But what a miserable hop it was. I landed on my forefeet and knees.

"Well, get up." The human's voice was angry.

I looked around for something to duck under. But again she didn't jump on me.

"You have to go back to the kitchen." She waited.

I waited.

Then she gave a satisfied smile. "You must have been brought in as extra help for the wedding. I thought so." She crossed her arms at her chest. "Well, you better learn fast—you can't come out here where I play. And no one is allowed to be naked. Everyone knows that." She frowned. "You're just a poor kitchen helper. You're ordinary." She tossed her hair. "I'm not an ordinary girl. I'm a princess." She smoothed the front of her dress. "I can't play with you. It wouldn't be proper. So go on back to your job." She flicked her hand at me. "Go on. Get out of here. Right now." She looked at me hard. Then she stamped her foot. "Now now now!"

I stared at her. This princess girl had gone mad. I watched her mouth for signs of foam. Mamma said mammals foam at the mouth when they're deranged. The girl's mouth was dry. But now her eyes were red and runny, like her nose. And here I was with no water to dive into and nothing at all to hide under. And I had grown so huge, I couldn't even hop right.

"Get up." She grabbed my elbow and tugged.

I found myself being pulled upward. Up and up, with my hind legs straight and my abdomen above those legs, instead of between them. I was standing on my hind legs. Standing. Just like the girl. A standing frog. Everything started to spin.

The girl's voice came a little less harshly now. "Your skin is clammy." Her face got a worried, pinched look. "You're sort of green, too. Is that because of the cut on your leg?" She walked around me and looked me up and down, pulling on her fingers as she went.

I had to turn my head to keep her in sight. My eyes were as strange as the rest of me. Most of my peripheral vision was lost. I teetered on my feet.

She took my elbow again and steadied me. "Your legs look strong. When you're not sick or hurt, you must be a good runner. Except your knees point out. And your feet . . ." She leaned over and studied my feet. "What a long fourth toe!"

Even dizzy as I was, I lifted my chin in pride. A frog's fourth toe is delightful.

She walked around me one more time. Then she stood in front of me. "If you were dressed and maybe not so poor . . ." She sighed. "Well, it doesn't matter. Off with you. You can make it to the kitchen alone, even sick." She lifted one eyebrow. "You can, can't you?"

I opened my mouth. A kind of choking twang came out. I closed my mouth. This crazy girl was right: I was sick.

The girl wrinkled her nose in distaste. "Well, I guess I can help you. Come on. Through this door." She went through the hole called a door. "Come on, Freaky Foot."

Freaky Foot? I thought she admired my toe. I wanted to leap away from this place fast. But I couldn't make it back to the well the way I felt. There was no choice but to follow this girl. I leaped—a pathetic little jump. Like a young toad's. Yech. But at least I landed on my hind feet this time.

"What did you just do?" asked the girl in alarm.

I hated to admit it. "I thumped," I said softly. Then I shook my head. The words hadn't come out right.

"You thumped?"

"I hopped," I said. There. That sounded right.

"Don't hop, you dunce. That's not good for your leg. Just walk. One foot at a time."

One foot at a time? That was unfroglike. But I couldn't leap, so I might as well try it. I put out my right foot and shifted my weight onto it. Then my left foot. I was walking. I stared at my feet. Walking!

"You're really stupid. Stupid and sick and naked, wandering around where you aren't supposed to be. What's *wrong* with you?"

I looked at the girl. She might be insane, but that was no excuse for being rude. First she called me Freaky Foot. And now she called me stupid. "I'm not stupid or sick," I tried to say. What came out instead sounded like "I'm not thtupid or thick." I moved my tongue around inside my mouth. My teeth had changed, too. Instead of being teeny things that barely protruded from my jawbone, they were big and wide and awful. And they went straight up and down rather than pointing inward, like they used to. My tongue kept bumping into them. I was hissing and spitting like a snake. And on top of that, my tongue felt odd.

"That's the worst lisp I've ever heard." The girl wrinkled her nose again. "Well, let's go." She turned and walked quickly.

I put my right forefoot in my mouth and tried to feel what was wrong with my tongue. Oh, no! Instead of being rooted at the front of my mouth, it was attached halfway into my throat. And it was shaped wrong—all lumpy and fat.

The girl stopped and looked at me. "Get your hand out of your mouth and come on."

Something was dreadfully wrong with my tongue. I stuck it out. No! No, no, no! My beautiful, long tongue, which should have been at least as long as my foreleg, was nothing but a stump. A disgusting stump.

"Don't stick your tongue out at me. I have half a mind to tell on you." The girl stamped. Then she marched off.

Who would she tell? And who cared? I stuck my tongue out at her back. But it wasn't much fun, with a tongue like that. I closed my mouth and followed slowly. I'd think about my tongue later. I'd think about a lot of things later. For now I had to learn to walk. Right foot. Left foot. Right foot. This wasn't too bad. Where was I? Right foot. Uh-oh. I fell.

The girl turned around. "Get up, clumsy. Hurry."

I got up. Right. Left. Right. Left. I looked around. We passed a hole to the outside, and I could see the field I'd crossed. My pond was beyond that field. Beyond those woods. My wonderful pond. My pond, which I had to save from the hag. Responsibility swelled in my newly huge chest. And with it came a renewed sense of confidence. Yes, I could save anyone and everyone—for I was The Giant Frog.

"Hurry. No looking out the windows." The girl snapped her fingers.

I took a last long look out the window, then followed her down tunnels and around corners till we came to a big room with a large fire in a sort of burrow in the wall.

A woman in a plain dress came up. "What is it, Mistress Sally?"

The girl spoke in an imperious tone. "I found this yucky naked person on the patio. On my patio."

I looked around for a human. There wasn't one. Crazy girl.

"Put some clothes on him," said the girl. "And keep him in the kitchen with you, where he belongs. This boy is not to go near my things." She pointed at me.

I took a step backward.

"Think of me for once. All anyone thinks about these days is the wedding. Well, I demand a little consideration." The girl turned and left.

I walked after her. Right. Left. Right.

"Hey, where do ya think you're goin'?" The woman grabbed me by the upper arm. "I don't know whose boy ya are, but if you're gonna work in this kitchen, you're gonna obey."

I stared at her. Work? What did she mean, work?

"So, and who sent ya?"

I didn't move a muscle. Were all the humans in this palace nuts?

"Hmm. Was it Thomas now? I asked that man to fix me up with some help. But they're comin' tomorrow." She bobbed her head up and down.

I looked at her in silence. Maybe if I was quiet enough, she'd go away.

"Well, I suppose Thomas wouldn't 'a' sent a boy so young if yer family wasn't desperate. There ya are, all naked. Ah, all right, I'll take ya. But ya better work hard. What's yer name?"

"Thimmy."

The woman seemed to think about that a moment. "All right, Timmy. I'm Kate. And you'll do whatever I tell ya." Kate squinted her eyes at my face. "Ya got the bile problem, eh? We'll fix ya up some gruel and you'll feel better in no time. All that green'll go away." She pulled me over to a round, flat thing on legs. "Take a seat on the stool, boy."

I stared at Kate. She kept calling me boy. And Mistress Sally called me that, too. I was a boy frog, yes, but it was strange to be called just plain old boy.

I looked at the round, flat thing. I was supposed to sit on that? I climbed up and gripped the front edge of the round thing with my fore-feet and bent my knees high and pulled my hind feet in close to my body. I was squatting on the stool.

"What're ya doin'?" Kate looked at me aghast. "That's no way to sit on a stool. You'll topple it over and tip the flour barrel. Ya don't want to do that now, do ya?" She pointed be-hind me.

I turned to look at the barrel thing. It was big. Kate was right; I didn't want to have any-thing to do with that barrel. I held tight to the edge of the stool.

"Put yer legs down. And look at that bleedin' cut." She slapped at my hind legs, and they dropped off the sides of the stool. She went over

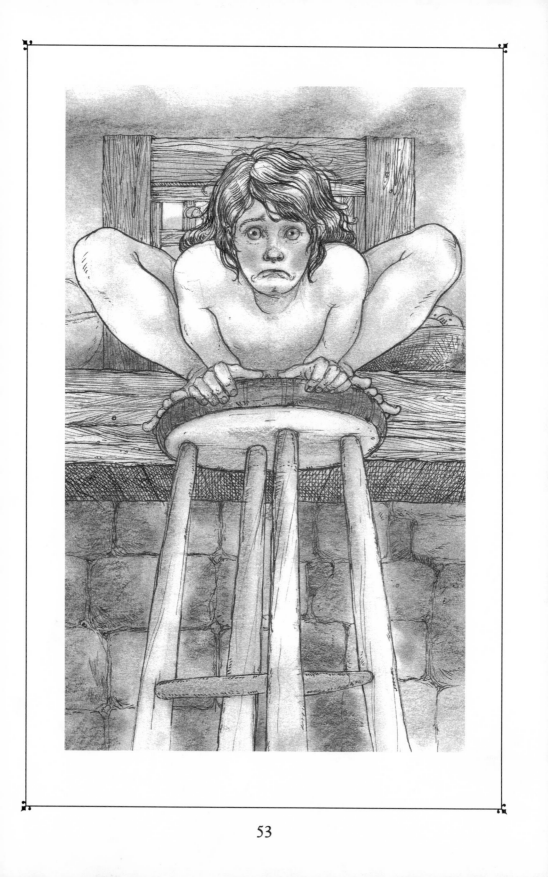

to a bucket and fooled around with something inside it. It looked just like the hag's bucket. I stiffened in fear. Kate brought back a dripping rag and took hold of my right leg. I pulled it away. She grabbed it tight. "Steady now. This won't hurt a bit." She scrubbed at the gash. It did hurt. It did.

"It hurth," I said.

"Well, what'd ya expect?" Kate went over to a wooden box and brought back a piece of cloth. "Slip this over yer head and I'll go find ya a pair of britches."

I took the cloth and wadded it up.

Kate looked at me. "Put the shirt on, boy. Over yer head."

I held it out and looked at it. A human's shirt. I put it on top of my head and peeked out from under the edge.

"What're ya doin' now?" Kate took the shirt roughly and pushed and pulled and jammed my forelegs around, and suddenly I was covered in brown cloth on my chest and back. It went all the way down to my knees and partway down both forelegs. "There now. You're half decent." She turned and left the room.

I examined my cut leg. It was already starting

to heal. I had long since outgrown the regenerative capacities of a tadpole, so I was grateful the cat Cashmere hadn't ripped off my whole leg. But I was still a young enough froggy that I healed super fast. By nightfall, that cut would disappear entirely. I got off the stool and walked, right, left, right, left, around the room.

That's when I saw the face of the human boy in a shiny, flat piece of silver propped up against the wall. I checked behind the silver to be sure. No one was there. So the face was a reflection, just as I had suspected. I turned around, but there was no boy behind me. There was no boy anywhere in the room. I looked back at the silver. The boy's face looked right at me. I put on my ferocious face and opened and closed my jaws a few times. The boy did the same. I shook my head. The boy shook his head. Slowly a thought began to form in the back of my mind. It couldn't be. I opened my mouth slowly. So did the boy. I snapped it shut. So did the boy. I looked down at my forelegs—but they didn't look like frog forelegs. The fingers, the nails, those protruding wristbones. I looked at my legs again. And now it all slowly came together—the hair, the separated toes, the teeth, the tongue.

Even the hot blood. Mercy. Could it be true?
Could Kate have called me boy because I was a
boy? A human boy?

And then the world went black.

F O U R

~ Stew ~

SOMEONE SLAPPED MY cheeks. I opened my
eyes.

"What are ya doin' on the floor? Did ya
trip?" Kate shook her head. "I never seen a lad
as green as you. What could Thomas 'a' been
thinkin' of to send me a sick boy? Ah, well. Put
these on." She held out more cloth.

I waved my forelegs in front of my face.
There was no denying it—they were human
arms. I was human all the way. And now suddenly I realized what had happened. The hag's
spell had done its work after all. I remembered

her flapping her arms and running in a circle. Yes. She said if she had her ring or if she had a princess to do her bidding, she could complete the spell. Well, Mistress Sally, for all her bad manners, was a princess. Mistress Sally had somehow completed the spell.

I was a human boy.

It was too much to comprehend. I closed my eyes again.

"I'll help ya," came the coaxing voice of Kate. I opened my eyes. She shook the britches in front of my face. "Come on. No more shenanigans from you, young man."

I looked at her neck and put both my hands to my own new neck. I looked at her ears and put both my hands to my own new ears. I looked at her bumpy chest and was relieved to find my own chest was just as flat and smooth as it had always been.

Kate pulled me to my feet. "Now hop on in."

I hopped. The britches flew out of her hands, and Kate fell over backward.

"I didn't mean *hop*, ya nitwit." Kate got up and rubbed at her back. She was a round woman with lots of padding, but the fall still wasn't so

pleasant for her; I could tell from her face. She picked up the britches again. "Pull 'em on quick, understand?"

I looked the britches over carefully. These were the things I'd seen on the man's legs. I nodded.

Kate kept rubbing her back. "One foot at a time, ya hear?"

I put in one foot, then the other. Britches were odd. They clung in all the wrong spots. No wonder humans didn't leap everywhere. Britches weren't flexible enough.

"That's better." Kate tucked the ends of my shirt into the britches. Then she took two pieces of hollowed-out wood from a cloth sack and put them on the floor. She looked at me expectantly. I looked back at her. "Well, step in," she said.

I stared at the wooden things. They were way too small for me to fit inside them.

Kate cocked her head. "Ya never had a pair of shoes, now, did ya? A real beggar boy. Well, these clogs'll fit ya."

Shoes? Is that what those were? But those things looked nothing like the pointed things the hag wore or the man's high boots. I didn't like them.

Kate scratched behind her ear. Then she got on her hands and knees and took hold of my ankle. She put my foot in a clog. It felt awful. She tugged at my other ankle. I fell.

"Oh, forget it. They'd probably just make ya trip more, anyhow." Kate stood and rubbed her knees.

I scrambled to a squat.

Kate pursed her lips. "Stand up, boy."

Slowly I straightened my legs. Standing was so strange. Even with my human body, I didn't see why people did it.

"All right now. It's time to serve the midday meal. Sure and you can serve a little food, can't ya?" She looked at me.

I tried to look agreeable. My fate seemed to rest in this human's hands. Besides, I sort of liked her.

"Ya can walk fine in your bare feet, can't ya? Ya won't wind up trippin' again, will ya?"

I shook my head. The britches weren't too comfortable. I stretched one leg, then the other.

"Well, good." Kate gave me a long look. Then she smiled for the first time. "Yeah, you can do it. Then after they've eaten, I'll fill ya up and see if we can get some normal color into ya." She turned and went to the fire, where she stirred an ugly bubbling mess. "The pot smells good, eh? There's nothing better than chunky stew cooked slowly in the fireplace. Let me just ladle out the bowls now. Bring 'em to me, would ya, boy?"

I looked around. Bowls? What could bowls be?

"The stack over there. Can't ya see well?"

I took a bowl thing off the stack and held it out to Kate. She ladled in sticky brown stuff. I stared at it.

"Well, get movin'. Through the door there."

The door was closed. I stood in front of it.

"Well, go on. Open it. Just push. And remember to serve the ladies first, eh?"

I held the bowl in one hand and pushed on the door. It swung open, then slammed back in my face. The bowl and brown muck went splat on the floor.

"What's this?" Kate ran over with a wet cloth and mopped the floor. Then she turned to me and cuffed my ear.

"Owee!" I pointed accusingly at the door.

Kate cocked her head. "A bit daft, are ya? Well, look. Ya push it open all the way. Then it don't swing back, see?" She opened the door. "If I've got to show ya how, I might as well do it meself and send ya home. Is that what ya want?"

I shook my head.

" 'Course not." Kate sighed. "Try another bowl."

Kate filled a bowl, and I carried it through the open door into a big room. In the center was a flat piece of a tree. And around the sides were three people, seated on stools with backs.

At that very moment the man with the horse walked into the room from the other side. My heart jumped. Did he have the gold box in his pocket? He sat down at an empty seat and exchanged greetings with the others.

Now I looked at the person beside the man. I recognized her, too. She was the first woman I'd ever seen in my life, if you don't count the hag—and hags aren't really people—the woman who had picked me up on the day Daddy disappeared. The woman who had almost eaten me. She smiled at the man in a friendly way and didn't look like an amphibian eater at all. But I knew better. Beyond her was Mistress Sally, who had stamped her foot and called me stupid. And the last one was an old man I hadn't seen before. No one even looked at me. I stood there, confused. What was I supposed to do now?

The horseman drew a circle with his finger on the wood. "I can't wait. I've been walking around the perimeter of the palace, and it's definitely time to dig the moat. The ground is soft with spring and—"

"Look at him, Father." Sally shoved a wooden box under the old man's nose. "Look at him now."

"Sally," said the woman, "I told you not to bring an animal to the table. And you interrupted the prince."

Prince? The horseman was a prince? Was that something like a princess? Like the hag talked about?

"That's all right," said the old man. "I'm not in the mood for hearing about your prince's plans for a moat again today." The old man lifted the top off the wooden box and peeked in. "So, Sally, this is your new friend?" He smiled into the box.

The woman leaned forward and peered in, too. "It doesn't look happy."

"I doubt animals can truly be happy or sad,"

said the old man. "Not in the way people are."

"Yes, they can," said the horseman. "Animals feel things just like people do."

I couldn't have agreed more. I craned my neck, but from where I stood, I couldn't see into the box. I listened closely: no hissing or scraping noises. The creature obviously froze when it was scared.

"Anyway, as I was saying," the prince said with a smile at the old man, "a moat is exactly what we need."

"We don't have any enemies," said the old man, waving off the horseman's words. "The only thing we have to worry about are thieves. What would we do with a moat?"

"Why, enjoy being surrounded by water, of course."

"Enjoy it?" said the woman weakly.

The horseman nodded happily. "Water all around. And we can fill it with pond creatures. Maybe even some water sow bugs, too."

At the mention of my favorite food, I jumped to attention and took an involuntary step forward.

The horseman noticed me. "A new kitchen helper. Hello." He smiled.

I tried to smile. The corners of my mouth twitched.

The man pointed to a spot on the flat tree piece in front of the woman. "You can put the bowl on the table here."

I plopped the bowl of gunk on the thing he called a table.

"He's the one." Mistress Sally pointed at me. "He's the one who almost made me lose it."

She was obviously still crazy. I had to escape her pointing finger fast. But not by leaping—I couldn't risk falling. So I walked, right, left, right, left, as fast as I could back to the kitchen. Kate handed me another bowl and turned me right around again. I walked back out, clutching the bowl. Maybe the brown mess in the bowl could be a weapon if Sally finally attacked me. The thought startled me. Frogs don't fight back. They flee or hide. Had my mind changed, as well as my body?

"He came and scared the frog away," whined Sally. "And I had to search forever before I found it again."

"Frog?" said the horseman, jerking forward, his face all tense and alert. "You've got a frog in there?"

I looked at the box in horror. A frog, like me. A prisoner. I remembered being a prisoner in the hag's bucket. I had flung myself against the lid over and over again, but it wouldn't budge. Poor frog in nasty Sally's box! I had to find a way to set it free. I crept up behind her, set down the bowl, and reached for the box.

The horseman reached at the same moment. Our hands knocked into each other, overturning the box.

The frog leaped high.

Sally swung out her arm, and the flying frog slammed into it and fell into the bowl. Brown gunk splattered across Sally's dress. "Ahhh!" she screamed. Now the horseman and Sally and I all grabbed for the frog. But it leaped from the bowl and landed on the floor—leap, leap, leap, going helter-skelter, as frantic frogs will. A toad will look before leaping, but a frantic frog is a wild thing.

"Stand back!" said the horseman. "Don't squash it."

"Get it!" screamed Sally. She looked right at me. "Get that frog, Freaky Foot."

I cringed. In a moment I was sure she'd bite me.

"Sally!" The woman stood up. "Don't scream." She looked at the old man. "Father, really, Sally's becoming a brat. And did you hear what she called the kitchen boy?" The woman glanced down at my feet. She looked away quickly, sinking into her seat.

"The frog!" screamed Sally. "Catch it!"

Without thinking, I dove under the table.

For a moment there was silence.

I squatted, unmoving, unblinking.

What are you doing under there?" Sally

leaned over and stuck her face sideways near mine. "You're acting like an idiot." Her teeth were big.

I didn't move.

The young woman's face soon appeared. She looked astonished. "Are you all right? Please come out."

I waited.

Next came the horseman's face. He had a strange look in his eye. "You're hiding, aren't you?"

Of course I was hiding. I waited.

The old man's face joined the other three, and all of them stared at me, their heads tilted almost upside down.

Slowly it dawned on me that no one was going to attack me. In their view, there was only one frog in the room, and it wasn't me. I came out and squatted beside the table. They stared.

"Stand up," said Sally.

I didn't want to. Standing made me feel like I was about to fall. But Sally's face was fearsome. I stood up.

"That's better," said Sally. "Now get my frog."

"I'll get it," said the horseman.

"It's my frog, and I want Freaky Foot to get it," said Sally.

The horseman frowned, but he turned to me. "Don't hurt it, boy."

The frog hopped madly in circles, unable to jump high enough to get out the window. I leaped toward it instinctively. But instead of covering a decent distance, I made one of those puny hops again. It was embarrassing. I walked as quickly as I could after the frog. I'd catch it and set it free. My heart beat fast.

I could see the bars on this frog's leg, dark and close together, much darker than any of my siblings' bars. Every frog's markings are unique. My stomach lurched—I was pretty sure I recognized those legs. I caught the frog and wiped off enough of the stew to have a good look. I stared. Sure enough, Gracie stared back. The little nut had followed me. This was very bad. It was terrible. Now Gracie's safety depended on me.

And my next thought was how stupid Sally was. She had gone back to the patio and found Gracie and thought Gracie was me. But Gracie and I looked nothing alike.

"Bring it here." Sally's hands were back on her hips again.

"Eccch!" screamed Gracie, but her voice was so soft I could hardly hear it. She struggled in my hand. For a moment I had forgotten I had become a boy. Gracie actually fit in my hand, just like she'd fit in the hag's hand only this morning. Yes, we'd both been at the pond only this morning—it seemed ages ago. And now here I stood with Gracie in my hand. Gracie—my friend—Gracie was in my hand. My head spun. The room went dim.

"Give me that frog right now." Sally stamped her foot.

I forced myself to bring the room into focus. The nearest window was only a few leaps away, but since I wasn't in shape for leaping, I would have to walk. Then I would dive out that window with Gracie in my hand and set her loose someplace safe.

Sally stood up. "Right now."

"No." The horseman walked toward me carefully, as though he didn't want to spook Gracie. "You can't keep her, Sally." He spoke without looking at her—his eyes were fixed on Gracie. "She couldn't live in a box." He took Gracie from me and held her cupped in his hands.

I wasn't sure I should let him take her. But

he didn't seem to want to hurt Gracie. And he was Daddy's friend. I had to remember that.

"What do you know?" Sally marched over and tugged on the horseman's shirt. "I can take care of a frog. It had a cut leg, and I fixed it. And who said it's a she, anyway? All frogs look alike." She swiped her hand through the air toward Gracie.

The horseman closed his hands around Gracie and lifted her out of Sally's reach. "No, they don't. This is a green frog. That's completely different from a leopard frog, which has spots all over it, or a wood frog, which has a black mask on its eyes and brown everywhere else. And a spring peeper has a big X on its back." A slow, wistful smile crossed his face. "All those frogs." He peeked through his fingers at Gracie. "A fine green female frog, you are." He lowered his hands and held Gracie in front of Sally's face. "See the white throat, the dark spots? Males' throats are creamy or yellow or orange. And see how her timpani are smaller than her eyes?"

"What are timpani?" asked Sally.

"These." He pointed. "In a female they're never bigger than her eyes. But in a male, they're always bigger. They're ears. We call them timpani."

"What do you mean 'we'?" Sally stuck out her bottom lip and lifted her chin. "Who's 'we'?"

The woman got up from her seat and stood beside the prince. "You're a born naturalist. It's one of your charms."

Sally hung on the prince's elbow. "Who's 'we'? And how do you know so much about frogs? I think you're making it all up."

"Sally!" The woman's face got red.

But I understood Sally. I would have wondered the same thing—only I was pretty sure I knew the answer: Daddy had given the horse-man lessons on frogs.

The horseman's face got as red as the woman's. He shook his arm free of Sally. "I like ponds." Then he looked at the woman. "The moat will be a kind of pond, Marissa. We can dangle our feet in it all summer."

Marissa gave a confused smile. "Dangle our feet in the moat?"

"It's all nonsense," said the old man. "You already built a huge bath and made us soak all winter. Now you want a moat."

"A bath is inside," said the horseman. "We need water outdoors. Just like this frog does." The horseman's face suddenly lit up. "Listen,

Sally, we can fill the moat with frogs. You can watch hundreds of them, all day long."

Sally clutched her skirt with both hands. She screwed up her mouth and furrowed her brows. Then she turned to the old man and said slowly, "Father, we do need a moat."

The horseman laughed and looked at Gracie. "Lots of little beauties just like this one will live in it."

Marissa put her hand lightly on top of the prince's. "You hold it . . . her . . . as though you liked her."

The horseman handed Gracie back to me. "I do. She was scared. I had to calm her down. She's young and inexperienced. And a bit too intrepid."

Marissa looked thoughtful. "The words you use to talk about a frog . . . You're the most un-usual man I've ever known."

The old man harrumphed. "Marissa, my daughter, the more your prince here talks, the more I suspect there's a lot of unusual things about him you haven't even guessed at yet. Yes, very unusual. I can't wait to see what his folks are like when they come for the wedding." He drummed his fingers on the table. "Come sit down. I'm hungry." The old man looked at me. "Put the frog in the kitchen and serve the stew."

"And bring Sally a fresh bowl, please," said Marissa. "She can't eat what the frog's been in."

"Stew time." The old man smacked his lips. "And when you're through serving, boy, take the frog outside and let it loose. We've had enough frog trouble."

"Never." Sally stomped back to the table and sat down. "Don't you dare set her free, Freaky Foot."

"Sally!" said Marissa.

Sally glared at Marissa. "You think you're so terrific just because you're marrying your prince in two days. Well, you can't tell me what to do. The kitchen boy can take the frog away while we eat. But then I get it back. It's my pet. You get everything you want. I want a frog!"

"You have to let it go." Marissa sat down across from Sally. "That's what the king said, and that's what the prince said. It's wrong to keep a wild animal."

As they argued, I walked quietly into the kitchen, holding Gracie tight. The problem was obvious, and I was annoyed. If I let Gracie loose here, that cat Cashmere might get her. There was no way around it: I had to make sure Gracie got back to the pond. And that meant I had to take her there. But I wasn't going back to the pond until I had the hag's crystal ring and until I'd found out about Daddy. So Gracie would have to stay with me in the meantime.

Just what I needed: Gracie to look out for, when I wasn't at all sure that I could even look out for myself.

Gracie. That pesky little frog.

FIVE

~ Kitchen Work ~

KATE PUT ME to work washing the stew bowls while she served dessert. I'd never washed bowls before. In fact, I'd never washed anything before. Frogs muck around in the mud all the time, but we never worry about cleaning off. Mud feels nice. And anyway, it dissolves away when we swim. And that was another thing—the water for washing. It was slick, and the bubbles made the inside of my nose prickle. Kate said they came from soap. Soap was clearly bad stuff.

I stood silent and watched Kate go through the door. Then I walked to the stack of bowls. I had to move slowly because, with Kate's coaxing, I was now wearing clogs. They rubbed on the top of my toes and weighted down my feet.

I squatted, picked up one bowl after the other, and licked them clean. I could have done it faster with my old tongue, but still, this new tongue wasn't as slow as I'd expected. The stew surprised me, too. I can't say it was good like glass worms or water striders. But it was tasty in a new way. And this was a better method of cleaning than soapy water. My hunger was satisfied by the time I'd slurped the last bowl shiny.

"Well, now, ya did a top job there, didn't ya?"

I jumped around to face Kate, and one of my clogs dropped off. No one had ever come that close up behind me before without my feeling their vibrations through the ground. It was the fault of the thick, ugly clogs.

Kate pointed at the clog that had come off.

I put it back on reluctantly.

Kate carried the bowls away. "They go here, on the shelf." She stood back and admired them. "A fast worker, that ya are. Who would 'a' guessed." She nodded her approval. "Well, Timmy"—she picked up a bowl as she talked—

"it's yer turn now." She ladled chunks of stew into the bowl and set it on the worktable. "Eat yer fill. I've gotta be on me way. Truffles, ya know. And decorations for the top of the cake. You're lookin' forward to the weddin', eh?" She laughed to herself. "We'll all get our share of treats, even you, Timmy. I'll see to that. You keep on workin' hard and I'll see to that." She patted me on the head and left, muttering, "Can't forget the candied almonds."

I poured the stew back into the pot, licked the bowl clean, and set it on the shelf. I looked toward the floor in the corner, where I'd overturned the small bowl with a loop on the side. I'd trapped Gracie under it. No noise came from it. I wasn't surprised. I knew exactly what Gracie's plan was; it was the plan any frog would have. She'd sit without moving until she sensed that the kitchen was empty. Then she'd try to escape. Since she undoubtedly knew I was still there, at least I didn't have to worry about her going anywhere for the time being.

So this was a moment of peace and solitude. I was grateful for it. I needed to think. Something drastic had happened to me. I was a boy. A human boy. The idea was staggering.

Only last summer I'd hatched. I wouldn't reach full size until the end of next summer. I hadn't had much adventure in my life beyond that one terrible imprisonment by the hag. And, it was true, I certainly had longed to see the world.

Still, I wanted to see that world as a frog. And I wanted to go back to my pond when I was through. I wanted to lead a happy life, wet and cold and free, as a frog—not a human.

A thin sheet of misery wrapped itself around my shoulders. I tried to shake it off. I'd better adjust and solve the problems at hand—and fast. I was Jimmy, hatched bold, a natural leader. The spirit of Daddy lived in me and would carry me through. It would. My family counted on me. The fate of the whole pond depended on me.

I squatted beside the worktable, my hands resting on the clogs. There was no time to lose. I had to get back to the pond within a couple of days. So what next? First there was the problem of getting that gold box from the prince. And when I did, I was determined to find out what he knew about Daddy. Then there was the problem of keeping Gracie safe until I could bring her back to the pond. And finally, there was the hardest problem of all: figuring out how to turn myself back into a frog. I would die of misery if I had to spend the rest of my days as a boy.

"It'll be all right. Just stay put, Gracie," I said over my shoulder. Actually, it came out as "It'll be all right. Thutht thtay put, Grathie." Gracie might not even have understood what I said, but it didn't matter. I was saying it more to convince myself than anything else.

"My name's Sally, not Gracie, and it's Mistress Sally to you. Stand up when you talk to me. And don't ever tell me what to do or not to do."

I jumped around. What was this habit of humans, to sneak up behind folks and talk to them out of the blue? I kicked off both clogs.

The girl stood in the doorway and pursed her lips. "Stand up."

I didn't move.

"Where's my frog?"

I shrugged. But I couldn't keep my eyes from darting over to the corner just to make sure Gracie was still there.

Sally's eyes followed mine. She ran to the corner and put her foot on top of the overturned bowl. "It's under this cup, isn't it?" She crossed her arms at the chest and turned toward me with a stony face. "It's mine. Stand up. You're annoying me, squatting like that."

I slowly stood and walked toward her. I didn't know what I was going to do, but I knew I had to get Gracie.

Sally put one hand out toward me. "Stop right there." She glowered. "All right, Freaky Foot. Forget what the king told you. This frog is mine and I'm keeping it."

I took another step toward Sally.

"Halt!" Sally's voice rose. "It's easy for them to say mean things like 'Frogs don't make good pets.' They don't understand. Marissa's had Cashmere for years, but I can't have a cat 'cause I'm allergic. The prince has Chester, but I can't have a horse or a dog or even a puny rabbit. I never get a pet unless I can catch one. And then, just when I love them, they die." She put out one hand and counted off the fingers on it as she spoke. "The garden snake. The baby robin. The big box turtle . . ."

My mouth went open. Then I snapped it shut. The girl Sally had killed a big box turtle. Almost nothing killed a box turtle, especially a big one.

"You don't understand. No one does." She

shook her head. Her cheeks were blotchy. "It's not my fault. Everything goes wrong. I put the turtle in a great huge bowl of water and I threw in tons of food. And all it did was get soft and icky and then it died."

A waterlogged, drowned turtle. Mistress Sally was a dangerous character. And she'd killed a snake, too. My skin crawled. I hated snakes, but the thought that Sally was capable of killing one terrified me. Still, it was my job to stop her from killing Gracie. I had to overcome my terror. Sally thought I was a boy, not a frog. She wouldn't kill me. "You kill thingth."

Sally blinked hard and pulled on her fingers like I'd seen her do before. "I don't kill things. They die."

"Frogth mutht be free."

"Not this frog."

"All frogth mutht be free. I know about frogth."

"Who cares what you know? This is my frog."

I took another step forward.

"Stop right there. I can have them flog you, green boy."

Flog? Did that have anything to do with frog? I took another step.

"I can have you thrown in the dungeon, Wobble Knees. You look stupid with your knees pointing to the sides."

Whatever a dungeon was, Marissa was right: Mistress Sally was a brat. Even the worst tadpoles weren't as bad as that. I took another step. Every fiber of my body wanted to squat and hop away, but I stood tall and still.

She made a snort. Then she charged, pushing with both hands right in the center of my chest. I fell. Sally leaned over and lifted the cup. Gracie leaped straight at her face. "Eeek!" screamed Sally. She jumped backward, tripped over my legs, and landed on top of me. Gracie zigzagged across the kitchen floor. The juices from the stew she had fallen in earlier had dried to a crust, and now they broke off, leaving a trail of brown flakes.

Sally got to her feet. "That's it. I tried to be nice. But you can't be nice. You made me fall again."

Kate came in the door from the outside just then, her arms hugged tight around a bundle. "Good heavens! A frog."

Gracie leaped past Kate, out into the grasses.

Sally ran after her. She stood in the grass and shouted, "Ahhhhh!" Then she turned to me and

put her hands on her hips. "You! You beast!"
Her bottom lip trembled. "You make everything
bad happen." Her eyes glistened. "You think
you're so smart. You think you know everything. I'm going to make you sorry. So ha!" She
marched off.

"What was all that about?" said Kate.

My eyes searched the grasses for signs of
Gracie, but I knew I wouldn't see any. She was
either far off or half buried in dirt somewhere

close by and wouldn't dare move till nightfall. I wondered where Cashmere was right then.

"Look at the worry on yer face." Kate put her bundle on the table and stretched a warm arm around my shoulders. "Don't ya take no account of 'er, Timmy. Just stay out of 'er way. Ya can see the sense a' that, can't ya? A good worker like you has got to have a brain in his head." She sighed. "Well, ya don't look any less green." She walked over to a shelf and took down a bunch of things and put them in a container. "Take this basket a' silverware and go outside and shine 'em up sparklin' for the weddin'." She handed me the basket and a piece of soft, almost fuzzy cloth. "And make sure ya sit in the sun. Sunshine's the best cure for the bile, don't ya know?"

Kate picked up my clogs and put them neatly, side by side, against the wall. "And it's okay for ya to be in your bare feet outdoors, sure." She gave me a gentle push.

Instinctively I leaped. But it was still only a little hop. I hung my head and walked out into the sunshine, carefully holding the basket of silverware.

SIX

~ The Trough ~

I WAS TIRED of rubbing silverware in cloth. And the hot sun made me feel strange. Itchy. I scratched at the back of one hand, and skin flaked off. I was drying out! Nothing could be worse for a frog. I had to find water fast.

I moved through the grass in long, rapid leaps toward the well. They weren't ordinary frog leaps. Instead, I pushed off on one foot and landed on the other. This method felt more and more natural. It allowed me to make use of my strong thigh muscles, so that I could move at a faster pace than I did with a silly human walk. I leaned over the side of the well, and the sweet moisture cooled my face. It was all I could do to keep from diving in headfirst. But no, I couldn't let myself. The inner walls of that well were smooth. There was a narrow ledge right under the waterline that any ordinary frog could leap from out of the well. But a boy couldn't stand on that ledge. A boy, even a boy with great legs for jumping, would be stuck in the well. I stared down at the water longingly.

Vibrations in the dirt. A man and a horse were walking up behind me. Trying to sneak up on me. Thank heavens I'd gotten rid of those ridiculous clogs. I panicked and leaped into the well.

The comforting water enveloped me. I went straight to the bottom to hide until they went away. But the strangest thing happened. My chest hurt. It started as a little pressure; then it grew until I felt my lungs would explode. I had to come up for breath. As my head broke the surface of the water and I gulped in air, I realized I was thrashing like a wounded frog. I kicked wildly, but I kept sinking.

"Watch your head," came a shout from above.

Bonk! A bucket hit me in the head. I sank.

When my feet touched bottom, I pushed off hard and broke the surface again.

"Grab hold."

I grabbed hold of the bucket and looked up, fearing the worst.

The prince pulled the bucket rope up, arm over arm. Then he reached out one hand. I took it gratefully, and he pulled me the rest of the way up out of the well.

I squatted in the grass and dripped, feeling utterly bewildered. I couldn't swim! What worse disaster could there be for a frog? And my lungs had almost burst—they wouldn't let me stay underwater.

The prince scratched his head. "Why'd you jump in the well?"

"To hide," I said softly.

"From me?" The prince looked at me hard. "You hid under the table, too. You're a timid sort, for such a big, strapping lad."

And now I saw my horse, nibbling clover behind the prince. The sheen of my horse's magnificent coat dazzled and soothed me, both at once. I couldn't take my eyes off him.

The prince followed my gaze. "So you like horses?"

I nodded.

"Do you ride?"

What a question. How could a frog ever get a chance to ride? I looked at the prince quickly, then back to the horse.

The prince walked around to the left side of the horse. "Well, if you won't tell me, show me. Come on. Jump up."

I didn't need a second invitation. I catapulted

right for my perfect riding spot: between the horse's ears.

But my human legs didn't propel me high enough. I landed with my belly on the horse's head, and I slid off the other side.

The prince ran to where I squatted in the grass. "Are you okay?"

I nodded again. I was confused but not hurt.

"Amazing!" The prince gawked. "I've never seen a person jump like that." He cleared his throat. "Your aim was off, though." He walked to the horse and patted the smooth slope of its back. "Try here."

That was easy. I jumped onto my horse's back. It was wide and strong. His muscles twitched and rippled under me. The realization of this creature's true power awed me. His dark gray hairs glistened in their silkiness. I leaned forward and gingerly touched the ears, mane, withers. I could hardly believe it was finally happening.

The prince handed me two long straps made of animal skin. "Take him through the field." He pointed west.

"Alone? Me?"

"Why not?"

I took the straps and screwed up my mouth, trying to figure out how the prince made that clicking noise that signaled the horse to go. "Ptu!" That didn't sound right. "Pta!"

The prince whapped the horse on its hind part. It took off. And so did I, backward, in a somersault over the horse's tail. Splat.

The prince knelt over me, his face pale. "Boy? Can you hear me?"

I blinked. Then I brushed at the back of my head. I wasn't used to having hair on my head (or anywhere else), and at first I jerked at the feel of it. Gradually I remembered everything. I got into a squat and dropped my arms by my sides. I was a human. And a bashed-up human: My head throbbed. But I was determined to ride that horse. I tried to look cheerful.

"You should have said you didn't know how. You could have been killed. Chester's the fastest horse around." The prince's voice rose with pride. "He's the best." He stood up. "No more dumb stuff, okay?" He puckered his lips and whistled like a thrush.

The horse, who was now halfway to the field, circled back and halted in front of us. The prince grabbed the straps from where they dangled loose on the ground, and got onto the horse's back. "Sit behind me. You want a hand, or are you going to leap again?"

I leaped up behind the prince.

He pulled my arms around his middle. "Hold on."

We rode. Slowly at first, making our way through the grasses, then down the path past the garden. The horse picked up its pace as we got closer to the field. The prince leaned forward, pulling me with him. That's when the horse took off again. He galloped. He ran. The wind whipped at my face. The drum of hoofbeats matched the joyful pounding of my heart. Even swimming my fastest, I'd never gone anywhere near this speed before. No condor ever plummeted so fast. No lightning ever flashed so fast. Faster and faster. Flying.

And then we were heading back toward the palace, and the horse broke into a trot. My breath came in heavy bursts. I was giddy. It had been better than my wildest dreams. It had been rapture.

The prince guided the horse past the palace. He stopped outside a big square building and slid off. "You coming?"

I jumped lightly to the ground and squatted, totally blissful.

"You look as happy as a frog who's swallowed a fly." The prince laughed. "Want to give me a hand in the barn?"

I straightened up slowly and nodded.

The prince led the horse into the building I now knew as the barn. It smelled of the tall grasses that grew near our pond—rye and alfalfa. Bundles of straw were stacked against one wall. The prince took a large piece of cloth and rubbed Chester's sweat-streaked flanks, while I looked over the row of other horses—five of them—all tall and strong, but none so handsome as Chester.

"Okay, let's go water him." The prince walked out of the barn. I followed happily. He stopped in front of a long, wide box full of water and patted the horse's side. "Put your head in the water trough. Enjoy yourself."

The water trough? It was barely deep enough to come up to my knees. But I obediently jumped in and stretched out full-length with my head underwater. When I lifted my head up, the prince caught hold of one of my ears.

"Are you nuts? I was talking to the horse, not you."

"Oh." I sat up.

"Get out, you crazy kid."

"The water feelth good." I stayed put.

The prince rubbed at his mouth. "It's true. Nothing's better than sitting underwater a while." He smiled. "And jumping is great, too. I used to be a fine jumper, like you." He nodded. "You wouldn't believe the things I used to do." He gazed off toward the palace. "No one would."

I looked, too, but I didn't see anything special. A long moment passed in silence.

Then the prince twirled around toward me with a grin. "Make room. You're hogging the water." He stripped off his outer clothes and stepped into the trough. He stretched out beside me, fully immersed. I watched the bubbles rise from his nose. After a few seconds, he sat up. He leaned against the side of the trough and looked dreamy-eyed. "I can't wait for the moat. You can soak yourself in it anytime."

I hoped I wouldn't be around by the time the moat was dug. But the prince was nice to invite me, anyway. "Thankth." A pair of centipedes crawled along the top edge of the trough. I snatched one and swallowed it.

"I don't believe you did that." The prince sat

up straight. He hesitated. Then he plucked the second centipede off the edge and swallowed it. He twisted his mouth. "They used to taste better. I hope pond bugs still taste good. Oh, well." He leaned back and closed his eyes.

I wondered why the centipede didn't taste so good to the prince. Mine was delicious. But I was too tired to ask him. I was tired enough to fall asleep. Still, I wouldn't let myself rest. The prince's eyes were closed. And his britches lay on the ground. This was my chance.

I climbed out of the trough and reached into the pocket of the britches. My fingers closed over the warm metal box. Yahoo! I jammed it into the pocket of my own britches. It formed a big, obvious lump in the wet cloth. I pulled at my shirt till it hung out over my britches. I turned around.

The prince was watching me. "A thief." He shook his head sadly. "A common thief."

SEVEN

ᕗ The Dungeon ᕕ

THE DUNGEON TURNED out to be a cold, damp place. Thank heavens for that, at least. Through the small window above my head came the gradually fading sun. It made a striped square on the floor—striped because of the window bars. I squatted in that patch of sunlight, fixed in thought. Every few minutes I moved a bit, following the square of sunlight across the floor. Hours passed. Eventually the sun set, and the dim glow of the moon made the room hazy. I moved to a corner and waited, listless and silent. All joy had left my life.

For one brief moment I'd had the box with

the crystal ring in my possession. Now it was gone. And Gracie was lost somewhere in the grasses, perhaps being stalked by Cashmere at this very moment. My mamma would probably never see either of us again. And the hag would return to the pond within days and dry it up. Everything was ruined.

I had failed.

And there I'd been with the prince all afternoon, and I hadn't even asked him about Daddy. I'd been so blissful over getting to ride my horse that I'd forgotten everything important.

All was lost.

Someone came down the stone steps on the other side of the dungeon door. Someone in clogs. My skin tightened. A hint of hope flickered in my chest; Kate had a core of kindness. Maybe, just maybe, she'd set me free.

The door opened. "I brought ya dinner." Kate stood in the doorway and put a tray with a bowl of stew on the floor. "Leftovers from the midday meal, but ya should consider yaself lucky to eat at all." She crossed her arms and frowned at me. "I could 'a' used ya in the kitchen. I told the prince that. I told him ya were a good worker. But 'e won't abide a pickpocket. And ya

can't blame 'im, can ya? I hate a pickpocket meself." Her eyes bore into me.

"What'th a pickpocket?"

"Why, you're a pickpocket. Ya stuck yer hand right in his pocket and took out a box, and don't think I don't know it. We all know it."

I looked away.

Her voice softened. "No bed, eh?"

"Bed?"

"Somethin' to sleep on. What, do ya sleep on the floor at home? Well, ya can't sleep on this cold stone." Kate made a tsking noise. "I suppose I could bring ya a blanket. Sure, and a pillow for yer head. Ya could use that, couldn't ya?"

I nodded. A bed. A pillow. Whatever they were, none of it mattered. I wanted to be free.

Kate stepped into the room, pulling the door shut. She walked slowly around. "I 'aven't been in this dungeon for years. 'Asn't improved any." She stopped short. "What's this?"

I turned and saw her squinting through the weak moonlight at the wall.

"Look at them spiders."

I knew all about the spiders. Before Kate had shown up, I'd been planning on having them for dinner.

"That's the biggest nest I ever seen." Kate's voice broke, and I detected a touch of fear. "Well, I'll just get me a broom and squash 'em. No one should 'ave to sleep with spiders, even a pickpocket." She rushed out, bolting the door behind her.

Well, that was that. Kate would never let me go. Would I grow old in this dungeon?

I leaped over to the spider family, intending to gobble them up before Kate returned and killed them. After all, there was no point in wasting perfectly good food. I plucked one from the nest and considered its plump abdomen for a moment. How could anyone hate spiders? But clearly Kate did; she was afraid of them.

And then the realization hit me: These spiders could help me escape. Yes! My hand darted out for a fistful. Yes, yes! I stuck them in my pocket. I swept another handful off the wall and stuck them in my other pocket. Then I went over next to the door and waited in a squat. The spiders crawled around all crazy-like, out of my pockets and up under my shirt and into the pits under my arms. They tickled. Hurry up, Kate, I thought.

Sure enough, muffled footsteps came down

the stairs. And they came none too soon. The spiders were crawling out my sleeves and up my neck and into my ears. Some had even managed to get down inside my britches. They drove me berserk. I could hardly hear, and I couldn't think at all. As the door opened, I pulled up my shirt and threw spiders on Kate. Only it wasn't Kate.

"Eeeek!" screamed Sally.

I leaped past her up the stairs.

Sally chased after me, shouting as she ran. "Spiders! You creep. Well, spiders don't scare me."

They didn't scare me, either, but their tickling was making me want to jump out of my skin by this point. I ripped off my shirt and threw it at Sally. Then I leaped for the nearest window and wound up in the grass outside. It was a magnificent leap. I was amazed and gratified. My frogginess had finally come through: I could make these human legs really jump.

Sally leaned out the window. "How did you do that?" She climbed up on the window ledge, swung her legs over, and plopped down onto the ground. "How did you fly like that?"

But I was already leaping away through the grasses, brushing spiders off me as I went.

"Who needs you, anyway?" screamed Sally. "You're nothing but trouble. And I caught my frog again by myself, so ha!"

That stopped me cold. Sally had Gracie again? I picked off the last spider and turned around.

Sally watched me. "That's what I came to tell you. I got my pet back in spite of you."

I squatted and worked to calm my voice. "How ith the frog?"

"Alive." Sally sniffed defiantly. "See? I don't kill things."

So Gracie was still alive. But for how much longer?

Sally took a deep breath. "I like her, this frog, you see, and I was going to ask you . . . because you said you know about frogs . . ." She scratched her cheek. "I mean, I wonder what I should do for her. For the frog." She rubbed her nose and spoke very softly. "I don't want this frog to die."

"Where ith the frog?"

"In my room."

"Free her."

"Oh, you're so annoying." Sally pulled on her fingers. "And I bet you don't know anything about frogs after all. You're a thief, so you're probably a liar, too. A nasty liar."

"Nathty? Me?"

"You've been nasty to me ever since I first laid eyes on you."

She was crazy. It was the other way around. But I wasn't about to argue. "A frog thould be free."

"Do you have stones for ears? I told you: I want a pet. I need a pet. Everyone else has something to love." Sally walked toward me slowly. "Okay, so we don't agree about the frog. Maybe we can still . . . I don't know. . . ." She sighed. "I don't think you're all bad, even if you are a thief. I feel sort of sorry for you."

I looked up at her. "Thorry for me?"

She looked back hard, as though she was examining me. "Why do you squat all the time? What's the matter with you?"

"Nothing." I pulled my shoulder blades together and stuck out my chest.

"What makes you green? And why do you point your knees out when you walk?"

I blinked. Sally would look a lot better if she was green and if she pointed her knees out when she walked. But I didn't tell her that. I blinked again.

"And why did you take the gold box? What could you use it for? No one would buy it from you. Anyone would know you'd stolen it." She stopped right in front of me. "It was a stupid thing to do. But I bet you're not really stupid. You act sort of . . . crazy. But you're, well, kind of fun. We could play together if you'd act right."

I looked Sally over. I doubted her legs were strong enough for a good game of leapfrog.

"I could get Father to pardon you, if you'd only act right." Sally scratched her arm and looked around. Then she bent over and put her face near mine. "Talk to me, please. I'm tired of your barely talking. I won't make fun of your lisp again. Please tell me. Why did you steal the box?"

Should I tell her? Was there any reason not to? She was acting nice to me now. She even said *please*. I spoke quietly. "I wanted the ring."

"Ring?" She straightened up and looked alert. "What ring?"

I felt suddenly unsure. I remembered Sally stamping her foot. Maybe it was a mistake to say anything more.

Sally folded her fingers together and pursed her lips. "Is the ring in the box?" She looked at me expectantly.

I waited.

"Is that all you're going to say? Oh, you're hopeless." Sally turned her back on me and walked toward the palace.

I leaped along behind.

She stopped and faced me. "Don't act like a fool. You'll wind up back in the dungeon. If the nightguardsmen catch you, it'll be worse for you because you already escaped once. Much worse. Run while you have the chance. I won't tell them I saw you, even if we're not really friends. So run. Or fly. Or do whatever it is you do." She turned and walked quickly.

I leaped behind her.

Sally stopped again. "Just what do you want?"

"The frog."

"My frog?" She threw her hands in the air. "No fair. Go catch your own. Now you better get out of here fast before they see you."

It was good advice—I wished I could take it. But Gracie needed me. I whispered my worst fear: "The frog will die."

"No, she won't." Sally crossed her arms at the chest. "I can take care of her even without your help. I'm taking excellent care of her, in fact. She's swimming right now in a pot of water."

A pot? Kate called the thing she made stew in a pot. I thought of Gracie, swimming in circles, wondering if she was about to be turned into stew. But maybe this frog wasn't Gracie. Still, even if it was some unknown frog, still I didn't like the idea of that frog being in Sally's pot.

"Give me the frog," I said.

"No. You're bothering me. If I tell the king you threw spiders at me, you're a goner." Sally walked along very quickly. "Go away. Get lost."

Worry made me wild. I leaped behind her. "Frog," I said. "Frog, frog, frog."

Sally turned again, and this time she balled up her hands and held them out in front of her. "Stop it. If you want the frog, you have to fight me for it. You want to fight for the frog?" She jerked her chin toward my hands.

I looked at my palms, white in the moonlight. I understood what she wanted: hand-to-hand combat. I'd never done anything like that in my life. But I knew about the mating grip. All male frogs know the mating grip. I leaped behind Sally and closed my arms across her stomach and lifted her into the air.

"Let me go." She kicked and squalled.

I dropped her.

Sally landed on her bottom in the grass and sat there, silent for once.

And that's when we heard the song. We looked at each other and listened. Then we moved together, without a word, as though the very song itself pulled us. We went through the grass and along the edge of the palace. We peeked around the corner.

The prince squatted on the ground with his face turned upward and sang a throaty tune. A familiar tune. It was a melody of rain and moonlight and insects and spring. It was a green frog's mating call. Daddy had taught the prince that call; I knew it.

The princess Marissa looked down from her window above. Both hands were on her cheeks. Her face showed bewilderment mixed with tenderness.

Sally thew up her hands and shouted, "The whole world's gone crazy!"

And I leaped away into the night.

EIGHT

~ Flour ~

I WENT STRAIGHT for the closest shelter—the barn. I leaped along to the spot where my horse slept peacefully standing up. I squatted in the corner and waited. My mind was numb. It was all too much for my frog brain. After a long while, I slept.

When I woke, the sweet scent of hay confused me. Then I remembered where I was. My horse stomped from foot to foot restlessly in his sleep. Maybe he was having bad dreams. I stood in that unnatural human way and patted his neck reassuringly. He opened his eyes, lowered his neck, and pressed his head against my bare chest. His muzzle was as soft as the pondweed that brushed my feet when I bobbed in the water. I scratched dirt away from his ears, picked some out of his mane. He gave a quiet snort of friendship. It felt good to take care of him.

Right now I wished I could be on the bottom of our pond, surrounded by fawgs, listening to Mamma tell a story about Daddy's heroic deeds last summer. But maybe I'd never be on the bottom of our pond again. Maybe I'd never be on the bottom of any pond. My human lungs couldn't do things right. Maybe nothing would ever be right again. But at least for this one moment, I could pick dirt off this horse. At least for this one moment, I could take care of another being, even if it was in a tiny way. The horse seemed to understand. He stood very still and let me groom him, this creature of beauty and wonder.

And I sang to him, at last. I had wanted to sing to him for so long, and after hearing the prince sing to Marissa, I could wait no longer. When I lived in our pond, I had dreamed of entrancing this horse with my lilt. My song now

wasn't like in my dream, though; it wasn't carried by my sweet green frog's voice—after all, I had no vocal sacs. But it was a trill, nonetheless, a trill that celebrated the smells of the barn, the touch of my cheek to his muzzle, the warmth of our mingling breaths. Chester pricked his ears and listened.

Finally I leaped my way out of the barn. The moon gleamed round and fat. It lit my path. There was still at least a couple of hours till morning, and I knew, with luck, I could carry out my daddy's wish—I could take care of the pond.

I leaped around the palace, on the alert for those nightguardsmen Sally had talked about. When Kate came back to kill the spiders, did she tell the nightguardsmen that I had escaped? I couldn't imagine Kate doing such a thing—but what did I really know about humans? Were they hunting for me right now? The thought chilled me.

I looked and listened. It wasn't long before I saw something helpful: a flower box in a window. The very window where the prince had been serenading Marissa. That was surely her room. And Sally's had to be nearby. I'd start there—I'd start by rescuing Gracie.

Heavy footsteps thumped through the grass. I flattened myself on the ground near the palace wall. An angular man loped along, swinging a thick stick in one hand. His lips protruded in a tuneless whistle. I was grateful for that ugly sound—it kept him from hearing the boom of my heart. I thought of the toad flattened on the ground, hoping the skunk wouldn't see him. I remembered the crunch of his bones in the skunk's jaws.

When the man turned the far corner, I went quickly to the kitchen door. It was locked. But the window beside it was open. I gathered my strength and leaped for the windowsill. But I leaped too far, on those powerful frog-boy legs. I flew through the window and landed on top of a mass of fur.

"Yeeee!" yowled Cashmere, as I tumbled off the cat and slammed against the table. Baskets of fruits and vegetables overturned onto both of us.

Footsteps clomped down the stairs behind the kitchen.

I jumped into the barrel behind the stool and sank into white dust.

"Eh? And what are ya squallin' about, cat?" Kate came into the room. I peeked from the barrel and saw her standing in the moonlight, her hands on her cheeks. "A right mess ya made, I see."

The door to the eating room swung open. "Ah, Kate. What's the trouble?" A short, stout man stood in the doorway with a stick in his right hand. It was thick, just like the stick the other man carried. So these were the hideous nightguardsmen.

I squooshed myself down into the dust, letting only my nose stay out in the open.

"The cat's turned over me asparagus and strawberries. Look at 'em all."

"Here, I'll give a hand cleanin' up."

"Nah, forget it, Michael. Sure and they'll still be here in the mornin', don't ya know. Can't clean up by the light of the moon." Kate made her tsking noise. "Just close them shutters while I toss the cat out the door, won't ya? Then he can't get back in."

I heard wood clatter against wood, and the door bang, and the cat yowl again. Then Kate's clogs clomped up the stairs, and the door to the eating room swung shut with a creak.

I waited.

The kitchen was silent.

I climbed out of the barrel slowly and picked my way across the room, feeling the edges of the table with my hands and trying not to squash too many strawberries under my feet. I stood in front of the swinging door for a long moment. What if the guardsman had heard me climb out of the barrel? What if he waited on the other side of that door ready to nab me?

My legs went weak. I wished I was back in our pond, stuffing myself on water sow bugs.

I turned my back to the door.

Then I thought of Gracie. And
ring. And the pond. And Daddy.

I turned back around and pushed c
just enough to stick my head into the

The guardsman stood by an ope
looking out. "Not a thing to re
Peter. Nothin' but the cat, probabl
mouse."

A laugh came from outside the wir
cat, Michael? Is that all?" He lau
"Well, can't say there's much activi
tonight, either."

Michael held his stick in his rigl
slapped it into his left palm over anc
as he talked. "Gonna be a good ci
weddin'. You should see the piles of
gatherin' in that kitchen."

I listened to the noise of the stick
hand. Slap slap slap slap. It was cor
ular. I bobbed my head to the rhy
could do it. I squeezed through tl
leaped, landing just as Michael's s
his hand. The slap hid the sound of
He swung his stick again. I leaped
right behind him now.

Slap, land. Slap, land. I was past the table
ow.

"All I want is me share of the puddin'.
Mmm, mmm. I love puddin'," came Peter's
oice.

Slap went Michael's stick. Leap went my
egs. Only a few more leaps to the open doorway
n the other side of the room.

"It's the roast that I'm lookin' forward to."
Michael lifted his stick.

I prepared to leap, one foot already extended
n that human leap way, the other foot on tiptoe.

But the slap sound didn't come. Instead, Michael pointed his stick out the window. " 'Mem-
ber the lamb at Mistress Sally's last birthday?
Ah, now, that was succulent."

I teetered, my arms waving about frantically,
my eyes on Michael's stick as he swung it up in
he air again . . . and finally down.

Slap, land. I stood on both feet in grateful
elief.

"The cake," said Peter. "Weddin' cake is
even better than birthday cake."

Slap, land. Slap, land.

And I was finally out in the hall. I turned the
corner and collapsed into a squat. The guards-

men's voices went on behind me undisturbed. I steadied my nerves and climbed the staircase without a sound. It was easy for me to find the right room; I have a great sense of direction. If only Michael and Peter would keep talking long enough for me to do what I had to do and get out of there.

The door to Marissa's room stood partly ajar. Inside the room I could see two long, narrow things. I crept through the door and looked more closely. Marissa slept on one. So that's what a bed was. It looked like an awful way to sleep. My eyes turned to the other bed. Sally's face was serene in sleep. Eureka! I looked around. A small table stood in one corner, but there was no pot on it.

I walked around the room. No pot on the floor.

I peeked under the beds. Aha! I knelt down and dragged the pot out from under Sally's bed. It made a small screech on the floor. I looked at Sally quickly, but she didn't wake. I turned to the pot. Poor Gracie swam wearily in a circle. I had to admire her determination; she was exhausted and she could have just stopped and floated for a while, but instead, she was still trying to escape. Her eyelids drooped. Her fore-legs flopped. I lifted her from the water. "Grathie," I whispered. "Grathie, it'th okay."

Sally sat up. She stared at me. She rubbed her eyes. She gasped. "A ghost." She threw back her head, and I knew she was going to scream.

I dropped Gracie, jumped onto the bed, and put my hands over Sally's mouth. "Quiet," I whispered, looking quickly around the room for the ghost. Marissa groaned, and I could hear Gracie doing wet jumps under the bed, but be-sides that, the room was still.

Sally rolled her eyes.

I was afraid she was going to faint. "Whith-per now, okay?" I took my hands off her mouth. "Where? Where'th the ghotht?"

"You," breathed Sally. Her eyes went wild. "They caught you and killed you and you still came back to steal my frog."

"Me? I'm no ghotht."

Sally pulled back and pointed, her finger shaking in the night air. She pointed right at my middle. "Look at yourself."

I looked down at my chest, white in the moonlight. All of me was pure white, all but my

hands, which I had dipped in the pot of water. I had to muffle my laugh.

"You can't laugh." Sally shook her head. "Ghosts don't laugh."

"That proovth it, then." I got off the bed and squatted by the pot. I splashed my face, and the white stuff turned gooey.

"Yuck," whispered Sally. "You're rotting."

I rubbed away the mess. "Thee? No ghotht. No rot. I'm alive."

Sally stared. "Maybe." Her voice was cautious. "Anyway, you don't seem too scary." She swung her legs over the side of the bed and leaned a slight bit toward me. Then she wagged her finger. "It's not nice to steal, alive or dead, even if you are crazy."

I had to agree. But life was more complicated than Sally knew. "You're right."

Sally gave a small smile of satisfaction. "Now catch my frog and put it back in the pot."

I nodded. I'd catch Gracie, all right. But I wouldn't put her back in the pot. I'd make off with her.

I reached under the bed. I couldn't feel Gracie. I looked. No frog. I looked under Marissa's bed. No frog.

Clink.

"There she is." Sally pointed in the direction of the clink. "Under my dresser."

Gracie sat there looking right at us, calm as could be. But something was odd about her. Yes, something was definitely wrong with her. Her mouth was wide and strange, as though she were making a human smile. The clink we had heard must have been something falling on her. Falling on her head. She looked stranger by the minute. And why shouldn't she? She was one sogged-out frog who'd been conked on the head.

All the same, I half envied her. What I wouldn't have given to be a frog again, even a dizzy, exhausted, waterlogged frog.

Sally looked at Gracie briefly; then she looked back at me. "Are you really real?" She pinched me.

"Owee!"

Marissa groaned in her sleep.

"We better go out in the hall," whispered Sally. "I'll catch the frog later."

Marissa rolled over, groaning again.

"Hurry up," hissed Sally. "You look awful. If Marissa wakes up, she'll scream bloody murder and the nightguardsmen will come and take you away."

There was no choice. I leaped out into the hall, with Sally right behind. She shut the bedroom door. I wondered if I'd ever see Gracie again.

"Well, you're in a pretty pickle now, but at least you're alive. I didn't really think they'd kill you if they caught you, but, well"—she shrugged and whispered, "you never know. And you sure looked like a ghost."

I gulped.

Sally touched my arm with one finger. She

smelled the white stuff. Then she licked her finger. "It's flour," she said slowly.

I waited.

"Why did you cover yourself with flour? I liked you better green."

"Tho did I." I squatted and sighed. But I couldn't think about me. I had to think about Gracie. "Free the frog."

"Cut that out. I won't set her free, and I won't talk about that anymore."

Gracie would die before long if Sally put her back in that pot. "Give her a rock."

"A rock?" Sally pulled on her ear. "Put a rock in the pot?"

"A big one. A dry one." One she can leap from to freedom, I thought.

Sally smiled. "Okay. She can climb on it. Then she'll be happy. A happy froggy." Sally looked at me.

I looked back.

"Thanks. You are nice, after all." She moved closer. "Now how are we going to get you out of here without anyone seeing?"

I didn't answer. I wasn't about to leave the palace. I still had lots left to do.

"You know, it's like I said before. If you

would act right—I mean . . ." She put out her hand and counted off on her fingers like I'd seen her do before. "Keep your clothes on, and not hop around all over the place, and stand straight, and not steal things, and stay out of the flour. Well, if you'd do that, then Father would pardon you, I'm sure. Then you wouldn't have to leave."

I didn't answer.

Sally cocked her head. "Oh, all right." She slowly squatted beside me.

I eyed her with approval. She wasn't half bad-looking when she squatted.

"I suppose you have to work all the time. I could tell Father I need you as . . . as my pet caretaker. Yes, that's it. You could have the job of taking care of everything I catch."

I looked away. "No thankth."

"It would be a lot easier than serving meals and washing dishes."

"No."

Sally was quiet for a moment. Then she stood up. "Well, it was just an idea." She pulled on her fingers. "So what now?"

It was time to move on. At least with a rock, Gracie wouldn't die. And I'd come back for her someday. All right. I looked Sally in the eye. "Where'th the printh?"

Sally screwed up her face. "Why do you want to know?"

"I need the ring."

"The ring again! You are absolutely crazy. You'd have even more trouble selling a stolen ring than selling a stolen box."

"I won't thell it."

"You'll never get the ring." Sally put her hands on her hips. "Never."

"What do you mean?"

"I'm just telling you the truth. Give up. Anyway, if you went in the prince's room, you could get caught again."

"Pleath, Thally, I have to tell the printh thomething."

She thought about that. "You want to talk to him?"

"Yeth."

"How come you want to talk to him but you don't want to talk to me?"

I waited.

Sally looked at me for a moment. Her bottom lip trembled. Then she burst out in tears. "You're mean."

"I don't want to be mean," I said, leaping in a circle around her. Her sobs were loud, and they made me nervous. "Quiet. It hath nothing to do with you, I thwear. I like you. Pleath," I said. "It'th important."

Sally wiped at her eyes. "You really like me?"

This wasn't a moment to reconsider. "Yeth."

Sally was silent. First she pulled on her fingers. Then she clasped her hands together with sudden resolution. "Follow me."

~ The Ring ~

SALLY STOPPED ABRUPTLY in front of a
door.

I smashed into her. "Thorry." I looked
around anxiously. We had crossed hall after hall
and gone down steps and up steps, Sally in the
lead, me at her heels, and the whole time I'd
been expecting guards to come out of the shad-
ows swinging thick sticks. My insides jittered.

"The prince is in there."

I looked at the door and felt instant gratitude,
and with it came a stab of guilt. Sally had led me
here because she didn't realize I still planned to

steal the ring. But I had a good reason for stealing it. The best reason in the world. If Sally knew about the pond and the hag, she'd understand. I had to believe that. "Thankth," I said.

"I hope you're not making a mistake." She threw her hands in the air. "Well, I tried to stop you." She gave a small, sad smile. "Good luck." She turned and left.

I went into the room.

The prince snored like a bullfrog. All my instincts told me to flee or hide. I worked to overcome them, for I was a frog—a frog-boy—with a mission. I looked around the room. The prince's britches lay folded across a stool. I leaped and landed lightly. I felt in the right pocket, the one where the box had been before.

It wasn't there.

I felt in the other pocket. Nothing. I rummaged through the rest of his clothes, which lay stacked under the britches, throwing them every which way. Nothing.

I leaped about, searching every inch of the room. Nothing nothing nothing.

"Is that you, Timmy?"

I blinked at the prince, whose eyes held me fixed. Caught again. This was surely the worst night of my life.

"Kate told me your name." His voice was low and steady. "I asked her about you when I found the dungeon empty." His eyes peered intensely through the dim light of early morning. "It was smart of you to come back. Fugitives are treated harshly. But since you came back, you can have your flogging and be off."

This was the second time I'd heard of a flogging. I didn't like the sound of it, but at least it wasn't a death sentence.

The prince sat up and put his hands on his knees. "What is that white gook all over you?"

"Flour."

The prince rubbed at his upper lip. I could tell he was trying to cover a smile. "Stealing cookies and you fell in the flour. Is that it?"

"No." I shook my head. "I hid in the flour barrel."

He nodded. "Of course. You're the one who's always hiding. Like in the well." And now he smiled openly. "We had fun yesterday." Then his smile faded. "Before you tried to rob me."

He slowly looked around at the mess I'd made of his clothes. Then he jerked his head toward me, and I could see the realization in his eyes: He knew I'd come to steal again. He got out of bed and felt frantically in his britches pockets. He took a deep breath and spoke, his eyes still on the britches in his hands. "Give me my box."

"I don't have it."

"Timmy, give it to me." His voice was angry now. "There's something important inside it."

"The ring," I said.

The prince snapped his head up and dropped the britches. "Did you take the ring out of the box? Timmy, you're making a big mistake." His tone was gruff. "That ring can cause evil. It mustn't fall into the wrong hands." He held out his palm. "Hand it back."

"I don't know where it ith. I thwear."

The prince put his hand to his forehead. "You know I want to believe you, but Timmy, you're in my room, and the box is gone. And you know about the ring inside it." He paced up and down. "What do you expect me to think?"

I could see his point.

The ring was lost. That meant the pond was lost. My whole body sagged in defeat.

"It's over. Give it up, kid. I need that ring. Now!"

No Gracie. No ring. And now here was the

prince saying the same thing Sally had said—telling me to give it up. But there was still one important thing I had to do. The most important thing of all. "Pin," I said.

"Pin!" The prince stopped in his tracks. "Did you say *Pin*?"

"Where'th Pin?"

"Where's Pin? Do you mean Pin?" He looked astonished. He walked around and around in front of me, faster and faster, half leaping now. "Do you actually mean the frog Pin?"

I knew it. I knew he knew Daddy. I knew it, I knew it, I knew it. I couldn't speak, I was so excited. I nodded.

"I don't believe this." The prince squatted beside me. He muttered as though to himself. "Pin. It was so strange that sometimes I think it never happened. Sometimes I think I just have a crazy imagination." He stared at me. Then he touched my arm. "You're not part of my imagination, though. You're real. But how? How do you know about Pin?"

"I athked firtht."

"You asked first? Is that what you said?" The prince pulled at his hair with both hands. He blew through his lips and shook his head.

"Where'th Pin?"

The prince licked his bottom lip. "Why? Why do you want to know where Pin is?"

"Thade thendth her love."

"Thade? You mean *Jade*. My sweet Jade." The prince dropped his face in his hands. After a few moments, he stood up. He walked to the window and looked out toward the well. "Send Jade Pin's love."

My heart sped. Daddy was alive. I leaped over beside the prince. "Where ith he?"

"Gone." The prince put his hands on my shoulders. "Tell Jade that Pin can never come back. But he's alive, and he'll be alive as long as I live."

I stared at the prince. Daddy was gone. Gone for good. Could the prince be right? I didn't want to believe him. But his face was sincere. His eyes were full of pain. "Long may you live," I whispered.

"And tell Jade . . ." The prince's voice quavered. "Tell her frogs are frogs and people are people."

It was a strange message. And it was wrong; I knew only too well. For I was frog and I was people.

Bang bang bang.

I leaped under the bed.

Bang bang bang. Someone hammered on the prince's door. "Open up in there."

The prince opened the door.

The short guardsman stood in the hall holding his thick stick. Marissa stood half behind him on one side, and Sally clutched the bottom edge of his shirt on the other side. "I've come to take the thief away." The guardsman came in, with Sally holding tight to his shirt, dragging along behind. "Where is he? It's off to the dungeon with the lad."

The prince moved in front of the bed. I couldn't see anything because of his legs. "You're wasting your time here, guard."

"Look," came Marissa's voice. "A white foot."

She was right. My sloppy human foot stuck out, white and gooky. I quickly pulled it under the bed.

Marissa's face appeared at my level. "Get out from under there, you thief. Get out right now."

I came out slowly.

"You look terrible. All pasty. Well, do stand up."

I stood up.

"Arrest him," said Marissa to the guard.

The guard looked sick. "Do I have to touch 'im?"

Marissa frowned at the guard.

The guard screwed up his face and reached for me.

The prince jumped to my side. He put his arm around my shoulders and drew me close. "This is Timmy." He smiled. "We were just talking."

"A chat in the middle of the night?" said Marissa.

"It's almost morning, and I'm an early riser. You'll see once we're married."

Marissa blushed. "Oh."

The prince looked right at the nightguardsman. "There's nothing for you to worry about, guard. You can leave."

"See? I told you." Sally jerked on the guard's shirt.

"Let go." The guard tried to wrest his shirt from Sally. He couldn't. He looked back at the prince. "I followed them white footprints up the stairs, sire. They went straight to the ladies' bedroom. And Mistress Marissa here, she told me the lad was a thief."

Marissa twisted a lock of hair around one finger. "Well, Sally admitted that he'd been in our room. Think of it. In our room! And then we followed his footsteps to your door. And I figured he came back to steal again. Why else would he have gone to your room?"

Sally shrugged. "You go to the prince's room. Do you want to steal?"

"Don't be impudent, Sally."

Sally made a monster face at Marissa.

Marissa held her hands open to the prince. "We have to lock him up. He stole your gold box yesterday afternoon, anyway, even if he didn't take anything now. We have to have a trial."

"No!" shouted Sally. She plowed into the guard. "Run, Timmy!"

The guard fell backward and bounced on his bottom.

The prince tightened his grip on my shoulder. "Don't go anywhere, Timmy."

The guard scrambled to his feet again.

"Sally," said Marissa, "you can't solve anything by plowing into people. That's stupid."

Sally stuck her tongue out at Marissa.

Marissa put her hands on her hips. "You're exasperating. Look, I like the kitchen boy, too, Sally. He's oddly endearing. But he's a pickpocket. Your friend has to stand trial."

"He's not my friend. And he's got a disease. That's why he's all white." Sally turned to the prince. "If you keep touching him, you'll die. And Marissa will catch it, too, and she'll die." She pointed at me. "Get out of here right now. Run!" Her eyes were frantic. She was trying to tell me something. I knew that as surely as I knew I was a frog. She was trying to warn me. I had to get free. I struggled, but the prince had me firmly by the shoulder.

The prince didn't even look at Sally. He spoke calmly to Marissa. "There's no call for a trial. Nothing got stolen yesterday, anyway. So we can just forget yesterday."

Marissa opened her mouth as if she was about to protest; then she shut it and went back to twisting her hair on her finger.

"Well, that's that," said Sally. She grabbed Marissa's hand. "Let's go back to bed."

Marissa pulled her hand free. "Are you sure nothing's missing now?"

"Of course he's sure," said Sally.

"Hush, Sally," said Marissa. She turned to the prince with worried eyes. "Did you check your closet? Did you check your bureau?"

"I checked everywhere," said the prince.

"See?" said Sally. "I told you. Let's go! Now!"

Marissa nibbled at her thumbnail. "Did you check your pockets?"

"Both of them."

Sally looked at the prince with surprise on her face. Then she looked at me. She was clearly troubled. She looked back at the prince. "Did you really check your pockets?" she asked in a small voice.

"Yes."

Sally knitted her brows. "You're lying."

Marissa looked shocked. "Sally! You are the rudest—"

The prince spoke firmly. "I checked."

Sally looked at me and chewed her bottom lip. Then she turned abruptly to the prince. "What about the ring?" she blurted out.

"The ring?" said the prince. He squinted his eyes at Sally. "What do you know about the ring?"

Sally twisted her hands together. "Everyone knows about the wedding ring. If it's gone, you can't get married."

"The wedding ring?" The prince laughed.

"You had me worried there for a minute. The wedding ring is perfectly safe."

Sally shook her head hard. "How do you know?"

"The wedding ring isn't even here. The gold-smith is bringing it tomorrow."

"But I thought it was in the gold box."

"Nope." The prince smiled.

"Oh, Sally," said Marissa. "That's so sweet of you to worry. And here I thought you weren't happy for me." She hugged Sally, who wrinkled her nose and pulled away.

The prince took me by the arm and led me out of the room, talking over his shoulder to the others. "Everything's settled now. You can all go away."

The guard scratched his head. "So I'm not to make any arrest?"

"That's right," said the prince.

"But where are you going?" asked Marissa.

"For a horseback ride. We love riding." The prince looked down at me. "Right, Timmy?"

TEN

～ Gracie ～

WE HEADED FOR the barn. My mind raced in all directions. The prince's gold box was lost. There was no doubt about it. He thought I had it; that much was clear. He had let everyone think it wasn't missing because he wanted to protect me for Pin's sake, for his friend's sake. And he wanted to get me alone so he could ask me how I knew about Pin. Yes, he thought I had the ring. I was sure of that. He had no idea where it was.

But I did. Sally didn't believe the prince had checked his pockets. That's because Sally knew the box with the ring was missing. And there could be only one way she knew that: Sally was a thief. A dirty thief. Oh, she might not have been all rotten. After all, she tried to help me escape from the nightguardsman in the prince's room. But she was definitely a thief. I wasn't sure why Sally had stolen the ring, but I knew she thought it was the wedding ring. She didn't know it was magic.

So now Sally had the hag's ring. And Gracie was lost. And I was a boy. And beyond all that, Daddy would never come back to the pond; at least, that's what the prince had said. I leaped along slowly. There was nothing left of all the hopes I'd had only yesterday morning.

"What happened to your shirt, Timmy?"

"Thpiderth," I said, twisting a little as I remembered the spiders crawling all over my chest and back.

The prince winced. "Sometimes you're tough to understand." He gave a small smile. "That's okay. What matters is that you should trust me. You have to give me back the ring. And you have to tell me how you know about Pin and Jade."

I sighed. This was going to be difficult. The

prince would never believe I was really a frog. How could he? How could anyone? I followed him silently into the barn.

Chester whinnied a greeting. The prince put a piece of metal attached to the reins into Chester's mouth. "The wedding is tomorrow. And someday I'll have a son. Timmy would be a good name for him. It sounds a lot like my favorite name." The prince looked at me kindly. "Timmy, my boy." Then he handed me the reins. "Lead him to the watering trough."

I leaped along, and the prince came right behind.

"Timmy! The skin on your back is splitting!"

I reached one hand over my shoulder and felt my skin. It was peeling away. I realized in horror that I was molting. Right here, in front of the prince. "It'th nothing," I said.

"Nothing? That's the worst sunburn I've ever seen."

I didn't answer. What did it matter? Nothing mattered anymore. I leaped out the side doors of the barn.

That's when I saw Cashmere. The cat was crouched down with his eyes fixed on the trough. He switched his tail back and forth. He

146

was ready for the pounce. I looked for his victim. And there she sat, on the top back edge of the trough. "Grathie!" I dropped the reins and grabbed her.

Cashmere gave me a dirty look. Then he walked off.

"Give me a look." The prince peered between my cupped fingers. "It's the same frog Sally found yesterday. Amazing! It's almost as though she's hanging around for some reason. But I'm sure I've never seen her before." His eyes darted toward me. "Have you?"

I nodded.

"So she's your frog." The prince pursed his lips. "You should set her free in a pond."

That was the truth; Gracie looked odder than ever. Her mouth was still fixed in that wide smile. Maybe being in captivity had made her goofy. If I hadn't come along, Cashmere might really have caught Gracie, acting all stupid like this. She had to get back to the pond fast, back to her natural life.

That was one thing I could do—return Gracie to the pond. While the prince adjusted a strap on the side of Chester's jaw, I dropped Gracie into my britches pocket. It was plenty roomy

enough for her, and she'd never manage to work her way out.

And now a new plan formed in my head. The ring was beyond reach. But my beloved Chester was here and Gracie was in my pocket and if I hurried, I could get back to our pond before the hag returned and, with Chester's help, I could transport all the fawgs to the nearest neighboring pond. We could race back and forth until the job was done.

The prince turned to me again, rubbing Chester's neck with one hand. "Tell me, Timmy, how did Kate ever find you?"

I picked up Chester's reins, trying to look casual. I had to fight the impulse to jump on the horse's back until I was sure I could really get away. "Thally found me."

"Sally found you? Where?"

"On her patio." I moved around to Chester's left side. That was where the prince always mounted.

"You went on her patio without her inviting you?" As the prince spoke, he held on to the little piece of leather along the side of Chester's head. "I'm surprised she didn't punch you right in the nose."

I wondered how tight the prince's grip was on that leather. "Thally didn't punth me. Thally kithed me."

"She kithed you. . . . Hmmmm. Oh! She kissed you!" The prince let go of the leather and pushed Chester's head up from the trough in one swift move. He stepped past Chester's muzzle and jumped around to my side and grabbed me by the shoulders. "Sally kissed you?"

Just then Sally's scream cut through the air. "He's got the ring!" She ran up, holding the gold box open. "Look!"

The prince stared at the empty box. "How'd you get that?"

"I took it last night when you went to bed." Sally shook her hands frantically in the air. "I thought it had the wedding ring. I was going to give it back. It was just to scare Marissa." She was talking so fast, spit flew from her mouth. "And I put it under my dresser and when I went back now and looked, the top was on the floor and the ring was gone." She looked at me. "Give it back."

But the prince barely seemed to be listening to her. He squeezed my shoulders and looked into my eyes and spoke fast. "You hid under the

table and in the well and in the flour and under
my bed. And you ate the centipede. And you
always leap along everywhere. And you squat.
And you're greenish, when you aren't covered
with flour. And your skin—why, you're molting!
Can it really be? Say your name for me. Say it."

"Thimmy," I said.

"Ahhchoo!" said Sally. "I hate your ugly
horse. And yuck! Look at his back. He does
have a disease, after all."

"Don't talk, Sally!" The prince let go of my

shoulders. His eyes were huge. "Jimmy. You're really Jimmy, aren't you?"

I saw my chance. I jumped on Chester's back, tightened the reins, and said, "Ptu," in my pitiful excuse for a click.

But Chester understood this time. He took off at a gallop.

"Jimmy," shouted the prince behind me. "Jimmy, Jimmy! I'm Pin."

His words followed me in the air. They panicked me. But I couldn't stop. I had to flee. Flee from the palace and the big, hard sticks and the people. Flee from those words. I leaned over Chester's neck and we raced. It was easy to steer him toward the pond. It was as though he knew we were going there. We practically flew.

Chester's gallop was smooth. Gradually the rhythm soothed me. Gradually the panic subsided. And now there was room in my brain for thoughts other than escape. I could hear Sally's 'ahhchoo' in my head. I could hear the prince's shout. He'd said he was Pin. Pin. How could he say such a thing? How could a man be a frog? How could a man be my daddy?

But then, I was a frog. I was a boy and I was a frog. And nothing was clear and easy. Could that prince be Pin? I remembered the strange look on his face when he learned that there was a frog in Sally's box yesterday at the midday meal. He spoke of species of frogs and the differences between males and females. And today he recognized Gracie, when Sally couldn't even tell Gracie from me—or she couldn't when I was still in my frog form. He squatted a lot, when other humans didn't like to. He ate the centipede with me. And he sang a clear green frog's mating call up to Marissa's window last night.

If he was Daddy, that explained how he knew about the ring. That explained why he visited the pond. That explained so much.

But that didn't explain why he had turned into a man.

And it didn't explain why he could love Marissa and marry her.

It was too much to think about. Too hard to think about. For now I had to keep my mind on only one thing: getting back to the pond and saving the ones I loved.

ELEVEN

~ Daddy ~

CHESTER WENT STRAIGHT for the shoreline where the prince always stopped. I urged him on, faster and faster—until I saw her. The hag! She stood at the water's edge and held a blue bottle in one hand. She was screaming something out over the pond. And she was swinging that little bottle around and pointing to it. I pulled on the reins with all my might. Chester paid no attention. He galloped right up to the hag and reared. I tumbled off into the muddy bank.

The hag spun around. Her mouth made a circle of surprise. "Who are you?"

Chester snorted and pawed the ground. I

stood up tall beside my brave horse, trying to look like a brave boy instead of a frog who wanted nothing more than to burrow down into the mud. "I'm Thimmy."

"Thimmy? What kind of name is that?"

"Give me that bottle."

The hag raised the bottle high over her head, and I knew I'd guessed right. The bottle held her potion for drying up the pond. "Criminy!" she screeched. "Look at your skin. It's coming off in sheets."

I looked down at my chest. The molting was progressing fast now.

"The sight of you makes even me sick."

"Give me that." I reached for the bottle.

The hag stepped back, and her eyes flashed. "Don't mess with me, ugly boy. I can turn princes into frogs. I did it once." She threw back her head in a cackle. Her wooden nose flew off to one side. She pushed it back into place. "If I had my crystal ring, I'd turn you into a frog this instant."

So this was what had happened to Daddy. I was sure of it! He'd been a prince. The prince I now knew. And he'd been turned into a frog by this hag.

And she could turn me into a frog, too. Now

I wished more than ever that I had that crystal ring. I was a frog at heart. I'd always be a frog at heart. I wanted to be turned back into a frog.

"But since I don't have the blasted ring, I'll just dry you up. Poof, like that. You're halfway dried up already, with that disgusting skin disease. But soon you'll be a total dust ball." She dangled the bottle in front of my face. "A perfect drying potion. Ha ha ha ha."

My mouth felt dry already. I had to find a way to get that potion from the hag. But first I had to set Gracie free, before she got turned to dust, too. One of us dried up was bad enough. I reached into my pocket and pulled her out.

Gracie blinked in the sunlight. She spit something big and shiny into the mud. Then she leaped into the water and disappeared.

"What's that?" The hag frowned. "A puking frog?" The hag frowned. She leaned over the thing that had come out of Gracie's mouth.

I leaned over, too. We both realized what it was at the same moment. But I was faster. In a flash, I held the mud-covered crystal ring in my hands.

"Give it to me, boy. Thimmy. Whatever your name is. Give it to me." Her cheeks twitched.

"Hand it to me nice and easy, without another thought." She held out her claw of a hand.

I was surprised she didn't try to grab the ring. Worry marked her gnarled face. She was afraid to snatch it. Why? I rubbed the mud from the crystal.

"Don't rub it. Don't! Just give it to me. Be a good Thimmy. Give it to me of your own accord. Don't think anything. Keep your mind blank." She showed her hairy teeth in what I realized was her idea of a smile. "Right here." Her extended hand trembled.

I stepped back and kept rubbing the ring. Its luster transfixed me. It was magic. We all knew that. But I didn't know how it worked. The more I rubbed it, the more it shone, until by now it glowed warm amber. This ring was dangerous. The prince had said it could cause evil. He told me it shouldn't fall into the wrong hands. The hag's hands were the wrong hands, I knew. She would do evil with it. But she would also turn me back into a frog. Could I bear spending the rest of my life as a boy?

Still, the prince's warning echoed in my head. It was my daddy's voice. I couldn't give the ring to the hag. I couldn't. No matter how much I

wanted to be a frog again. I squeezed the ring tight and wished:

Oh, if only this ring could make each of us who touched it what we really are at heart.

Zap! The ring dropped from my hand. It sat in front of me on the mud, and beside it lay a frog's molted skin as clear as day, and beyond that was a pair of empty britches. I looked up at the hag, who was now amazingly tall. I looked down at my creamy yellow belly; at my smooth, wet, hairless new skin; at my webbed hind feet and the glorious olive green bars on my legs. I was me! I was a frog again!

"What!" The hag leaned over me. "I turned you into a frog just by saying it. Yahoo! Look at that. I didn't even have to rub the crystal ring and wish. I did it with my own words." She grinned hideously. "I'm more powerful than ever. I can do transformations with or without the ring." The hag danced around and around in the mud.

"Ha ha ha ha. The thrill of it! I've got to do it again. What fun! I'll turn you into a newt. There. Change!" She stared at me expectantly.

I looked down again, but my body stayed frog, wonderful green frog. I was a frog and I'd never be anything other than a frog again. I filled my left vocal sac and croaked in glee.

But my croak was cut off as the hag grabbed me around my middle. "You infernal frog. I'll make you a newt, all right." She tightened her grip. I could barely breathe. She furrowed her thick brows until there was one continuous, bushy line across her forehead. Then she made a slow, smelly, hateful smile. "I'll change you into a newt with the ring. This ring hasn't been wished on since way last summer. But I'm sure its powers haven't gone stale. It's time for a fresh wish." She slipped her finger into the crystal ring.

And Zap! I was sitting on top of a big, cold iron rock. The crystal ring glowed on one side of me, and a wooden nose rested on the other side. At the foot of the rock was a pile of rags that I recognized as the hag's clothes. Chester whinnied and ran off into the field.

I felt just as startled as Chester. I quickly dove into the water. I swam for the reeds and found my zillions of siblings bobbing around there.

"She's gone," said a fawg.

"Where?" said another.

"Who cares?" said a third.

"The hag's gone," they sang together. "The pond's saved." The air was filled with happy croaking. It was deafening. Anyone would have thought it was a month later and the green frogs were all mating.

I didn't croak, though. I was already thinking

ahead. How was I going to explain to Mamma that Daddy was now a prince? How was I going to tell her that he was alive, but he'd never come back to the pond?

Gracie came up beside me. "Dreamer, am I glad to see you. I thought you were dead."

"How could you think I was dead?" I shouted over the din of the croaking. "I saved you."

"Don't be absurd. That nice green-and-white boy saved me."

"Gracie, I was that boy."

Gracie shot out her tongue and ate a black fly. "Dreamer, are you going to talk crazy all your life?" She bobbed over closer. "Do you want attention? You're jealous, aren't you?"

"Jealous? Of what?"

Gracie swam around me. "You are. You're jealous because I'm the one who brought back the hag's ring, not you. I'm the one who saved the pond."

I opened my mouth to protest, but just at that moment the croaking ceased. Silence fell across the pond. Someone must have sensed danger and stopped croaking. Whenever one frog stops croaking, all frogs stop.

And now I could see what it was. The prince rode up on a bay horse. I recognized it from the barn. He slid off the horse, picked up my old britches, and shook them. He looked around. "What's this big iron rock? It was never here be- fore." He walked to the rock and stared down at the pile of the hag's clothes. Then his eye fixed on the ring. But he didn't pick it up. He turned and looked out over the pond. "Jimmy?" he called. "Jimmy, are you there?"

His call pierced my heart. Should I go to him? I could feel the eyes of my siblings on me. They wondered how this prince had learned my name. They didn't know he was Daddy. I gave a small croak.

The prince walked to the very edge of the water. "I heard you." His eyes searched among the reeds. "I heard you, child." Then he looked again at the ring.

I remembered my wish. I had been holding the ring when I made it. I had wished that the ring would turn each of us who touched it into what we really are at heart. The hag had been worried when I held the ring. She told me not to think. And yes, that was it! My wish had worked. The ring had turned me into a frog.

The ring had turned the hag into an iron rock. It was all because of the ring—the power of the ring. And my wish was still fresh in that ring. What would happen if the prince touched the ring? Would the ring turn him into Pin again? Was my daddy a frog at heart?

The prince looked at the ring for a long time. I thought of shouting to him. I thought of telling him what it would mean if he touched it. But I stayed silent. I felt barely alive. It was as though I were suspended between life and death, suspended by my great desire to have Pin back.

Finally, the prince looked out at the pond again. "You used the ring to turn back into yourself, didn't you? That was smart. You always were smart, Jimmy. So now what? Should I leave the ring here? Will you need it again?" He looked around. Then he spied the blue bottle. "What's this?" He opened it and sniffed.

For one awful moment I thought he might drink it. I forced myself into action. I swam toward him as fast as I could, but I knew I'd never be able to knock it out of his hands in time. He closed the bottle and slipped it into his pocket. I stopped swimming and floated in relief, bobbing against the reeds.

Next he picked up the wooden nose. "This is even weirder." He shook his head, but he put the nose into his pocket, too. "Look, Jimmy. I've got to go. Can you understand that?" He looked right toward me, but I knew he couldn't see me in the reeds. His face was tormented. "I can hardly understand it myself."

My thin new skin burned at his words.

"If you ever decide you want to live with me, you know where to find me. You're part boy." Daddy extended both hands. "All of you out there, all of you fawgs, I'll always welcome you. Remember that." He rubbed his chin. "I'll take the ring, so that it doesn't fall into the wrong hands. You know where to get it if you ever need it." He reached out his hand toward the ring.

I held my breath.

And then he picked up the ring.

Nothing changed.

My daddy, Pin, the prince—he was a man at heart.

He grabbed the reins of the other horse and whistled. Chester came trotting up.

And through my tears, I watched the prince mount and ride away, leading the other horse behind.